where EVIL walks

C.M. CURTIS

kwympublishing.com
info@kwympublishing.com

1st Edition
Cover Design/Page Layout by KWYM Publishing

ISBN-13: 9781973172475

DEDICATION

To my family, and all my friends.

CONTENTS

CHAPTER 1

Even though it was a new coffin, the hinges creaked eerily as Ed Macon lifted the lid. A tremor ran through his big body at the thought of what he was doing, and he almost dropped the candle he was holding. "I ain't ever done a thing like this before, Priscilla."

He leaned the lid of the elegant coffin back against the wall of the mausoleum, intentionally not looking at the body inside. He said, "I'm not sure we should do this."

Priscilla set her candle on the edge of the coffin, moved over to him, and pushed herself up against him, turning her face upward. "I know, sweetheart. It's hard for me, too; that's why I asked you to help me. You're the one I can always rely on. You're the only person I've ever known who I could always trust." She pulled his head down and pressed her lips to his in a long kiss, after which she laid her head on his chest. "Oh, my love," she said in a half whisper, "I'm so glad I've found you. I've needed you for as long as I can remember."

After a while, she pulled away from him and said, in a cheerful voice, "Let's finish this and go get married."

He grinned and said, "And then can we tell folks? I don't understand why we've had to keep it a secret."

"I guess it's my superstition. I just didn't want anyone to know about us until after we're married, for fear something would spoil it. You haven't told anyone, have you?"

"Not a soul, honey. But I'll shout it to the world after we're hitched."

"Well, then, let's get this done and get on over to the preacher's house," Priscilla said cheerily.

He laughed in pure joy. "It's one o'clock in the morning."

"I don't care. We'll wake him up." She seemed to be nearly dancing with gleeful anticipation.

Priscilla's stepmother had been a corpulent woman, and, despite his large size and farmer's strength, it was not without difficulty that

Ed Macon lifted her body from the coffin and laid it on the stone floor of the mausoleum. They carried the empty coffin outside in the darkness, setting it in the back of Ed's wagon, after which Ed lifted a high-backed, wooden chair out of the wagon and carried it inside.

"Set it against that wall," said Priscilla, pointing.

Ed complied and went back outside, returning a short time later, carrying a large, framed portrait. Priscilla took the portrait from him and said, "Put her in the chair."

In the dim candlelight, she saw Ed make a face of disgust, but, grunting, he lifted the big body from the floor and set it in the chair. "She was a big one," he said.

"That's why I needed a big, strong man like you to help me with this," said Priscilla.

"After tonight, you'll have me always, honey."

Priscilla hung the portrait from a hook set in the opposite wall, straightened it, and stepped back. The hook had been put there by the stonemason whom Priscilla's stepmother had contracted to build this mausoleum while she was still suffering from the mysterious illness that had finally killed her. After the woman had become too ill to direct the project, Priscilla had taken over and, though she was not the one paying for the work, had added some details of her own design to the structure. One of them was the hook from which the portrait was now hanging.

Priscilla straightened the picture and reached into her deep pocket for the long pieces of stout cord she had brought. Using the cord, she bound her stepmother's body to the chair and tied her head back so it faced forward.

Observing this, Ed said, "Honey, I don't understand this. Seems awful queer to me."

Reaching into her pocket, Priscilla turned and faced him, smiling. She went to him, and he—horribly misinterpreting her intentions—held out his arms to embrace her. As he did, she plunged the knife into his abdomen.

Ed's reaction was not what Priscilla had anticipated. Instead of falling to the floor, he screamed and lashed out, thrusting her away from him. He stood there for a moment, facing her, a look of intense hurt on his face. He pulled the knife out and looked at it. It glistened with his blood. Suddenly, his hurt expression was replaced by one of anger. He bellowed a curse at her and moved toward her, holding the knife.

The little gun appeared in her hand as if out of nowhere, and she fired both barrels at point-blank range. This time, Ed dropped to the floor, and in a few seconds, he was as dead as the woman in the chair.

Priscilla retrieved her knife, wiped it on Ed's shirt, and returned it to the sheath in her pocket. Ignoring Ed's body, she went to the corpse of her stepmother and, after pinning the eyes open, pointed to the portrait on the opposite wall, and said in a voice filled with venom, "You hated that portrait so much. Well, now you can look at it for eternity, you old cow."

Leaving Ed's body where it had fallen, Priscilla went outside and wrestled the coffin out of the wagon bed, allowing it to fall on the ground. She dragged it inside the mausoleum, laid it partially on top of Ed's body, and left it there. She went back out and closed the heavy iron door of the mausoleum. Taking a large and intricately fashioned key from her pocket, she locked the special lock she had ordered from a company in New York, went to the wagon, and climbed up onto the seat.

She drove to Ed's farm and there unhitched the horses, turning them into their pasture. She went inside Ed's house, lit a candle, and looked at the little pocket watch she carried. It was just past two a.m. She found the coffee can where Ed had kept his money, and emptied it into her pocket. She looked around and, deciding there was nothing more there she wanted, left the house on foot.

A mile down the road, she came to the bridge. Halfway across, she took from her pocket the two keys to the door of the mausoleum and, without any hesitation, threw them into the river.

CHAPTER 2

"**Y**ou killed a woman, and you think I should let you go?" It was Marshal Pitts who was talking to the tall, well-dressed man who sat in a loose, stretched-out fashion on one of the chairs in the marshal's office, showing no more concern at being handcuffed to the chair than if he had been drinking a beer in his favorite saloon.

"I think you should give me a medal," the man said.

The marshal scowled. "Mister, I don't know where you come from, but—"

"Up until about a year ago, from Las Cruces," interrupted the lean man. "My name is Earl Sutherton. You might have heard of me."

The marshal tried unsuccessfully not to show his shock at this pronouncement. He opened his mouth, but Sutherton beat him to the verbal draw and said, "Figured you would've heard of me, you being a lawman."

"I've heard of you all right, but I never heard tell of you killin' a woman."

"That's because in those days, I was a bad man, and my actions were evil ones. Not too long ago, I decided to change. Got tired of the wild life, all the fighting and killing and hating."

Marshal Pitts rubbed his red beard and shook his head. "Seems to me like you've got somethin' twisted crosswise in your skull if you think goin' straight means killin' women."

Sutherton gave an ironic smile, started making a cigarette with his un-fettered hand, and said, "One of the few good things I've done in my life." He paused to lick the paper and put the cigarette between his lips, but he made no attempt to light it. He said, "There's a whole long story behind this thing. You might like to hear it."

"I would thoroughly love to," said the marshal, with no small amount of condescension. "Not that anything you could say will save your neck from a rope."

4

The comment had no noticeable effect on Sutherton. He asked, "You got a judge in this town?"

"We surely do, and you'll be meetin' him right soon, I can promise you that."

"What's his name?"

"Judge Markham, not that it matters."

Sutherton smiled and looked away, and the marshal thought there was something of satisfaction, or perhaps relief in his smile. Sutherton said in a soft voice, "I want to talk to him."

"You'll get your chance, tomorrow mornin' at the arraignment."

"Tonight."

"Listen, Sutherton, you ain't the one who decides—"

Sutherton interrupted again, "Marshal, don't you think it's a little strange that a man with my reputation as a gunfighter would show up in your town, kill a woman, and then come to your office, tell you where to find the body, and turn himself in? What if I hadn't handed you my gun? What if you had been forced to come after me—to draw down on me?"

Sutherton looked directly into the marshal's eyes, holding his gaze until the man finally looked away, and for a long moment, neither man spoke. There was no need.

Presently, Sutherton said, "I had my reasons for doing what I did. All I'm asking is to be allowed to tell my story, and if you want to hear it, you'll have to go get Judge Markham. Otherwise, you'll never hear another peep out of me."

The marshal seemed to consider this for a few moments, and then he turned and left the office, locking the door from the outside. When he returned, he was accompanied by a short, pudgy, bald man in a rumpled, gray suit. The man appeared to be in his early sixties. He looked at Sutherton severely, and said, "I'm Judge Markham. Marshal Pitts here has told me the whole story. He says you wanted to see me."

Sutherton said, "I'll have to respectfully correct you on one point, Your Honor. You haven't heard the whole story. You haven't heard more than a tiny part of it, but if you would be so kind as to indulge me, I'll tell you the rest of it."

Judge Markham pulled out his watch and looked at it. "All right, but keep it short. It's supper time."

Sutherton smiled in a way that said he knew something that gave him the upper hand, but he made no comment. The unlighted cigarette was still between his lips. His expression became sober, and he began speaking.

"A while back, I was working in New Mexico for a man who was rich and wanted to be richer. There was some killing involved, and when it was done, I was sick of it. The man paid me a lot of money, and I stole a lot more under circumstances that don't matter here, so I won't talk about them."

The judge and the marshal exchanged a glance, but neither of them saw fit to interrupt the story.

"I already had a goodly sum of money saved up before I took that job," continued Sutherton, "and when I combined the three piles of money, I realized there was no more reason for me to go on working."

"You mean go on killing," said the judge.

"That was my line of work, Your Honor. I'm not denying anything. Anyhow, I changed my name and bought a house on some land, near a town that's a good five hundred miles from here. The name of the town and exactly where it's located are not important. The place I bought is a nice, quiet little place. It's secluded; that's what I like best about it. I acquired a couple of dogs, some horses, a few steers, and a milk cow. For the first time in my life, I had found peace."

Judge Markham looked at his watch again, and then he dragged a chair over from the far wall and sat down, facing the prisoner. The marshal followed suit, and the judge said, "Go on."

"It all began—at least my part of it did—when a woman who called herself Lorna Madsen married a rancher named Saul Fergin and became Lorna Fergin. After that, a lot of people had a lot of trouble. One of them was a man named Nate Tennet, a rancher near where I live. Two others were a couple of young farm boys."

"Is there some reason why this should be of interest to us?" asked Judge Markham.

Sutherton looked at him for a moment and simply answered, "Absolutely."

CHAPTER 3

Nate Tennet stepped into Ballenger's saloon and right into trouble. The habitual grin he wore on his face remained intact, showing just how little regard he had for the men of the Lazy 8, who had clearly been waiting for him and now surrounded him.

Tennet said, "I guess you ladies figure it'll take all of you to do this job. Hope you brought your hankies, because I'm going to bloody some noses." And, with this, he charged the two men nearest him, taking them off guard and knocking them both to the floor. He wheeled and hit squarely in the face the first man charging him, and then he was surrounded by Lazy 8 riders, none of whom had any intention of allowing him to leave this room standing up.

When it was over, and the hard-breathing men had backed off, leaving Tennet lying on the floor, battered and bloody, Dale Ramsey, foreman of the Lazy 8, stood over him and said, "Could have been a lot worse, Tennet. That was just a warning."

"Somebody needs to warn you, too, Ramsey," wheezed Tennet, wincing as he pulled himself to a sitting position. "Don't ever let me catch you alone without your protectors."

The comment had its effect, and Tennet saw it on Ramsey's face. But there was nothing the foreman could do about it. To further punish Tennet in his beaten condition would only prove Tennet's point for him. Ramsey wheeled and tramped out to the street. The others followed him, and soon Tennet heard the sounds of the Lazy 8 men riding away. He pulled himself to his feet, staggered to the bar, and leaned heavily on it. "Still got that scattergun under there, Cecil?" he asked the bar man in a hoarse voice.

"Yes," said Cecil, noncommittally. Then he said, "On me," as he poured a drink for Tennet.

"Let me see it," ordered Tennet.

"You ain't goin' to . . ."

Tennet's voice was hard, and his eyes sent their warning to Cecil. "Let me see it."

With obvious reluctance, Cecil produced the sawed-off shotgun.

Tennet made no move to take the shotgun; he just nodded, and Cecil quickly put the weapon away.

"You've sold your last drink to any Cross T man," said Tennet, pushing away the drink Cecil had set in front of him.

"Now, Nate. That's awful hard. I had no choice . . ."

Tennet cut him off. Clutching the edge of the bar to keep from falling, he said, "I'll tell you somethin', Cecil. A fence-sitter is the worst kind of coward. Sooner or later, every man will declare where he stands, either by taking action, or by doing nothing. You just did."

"Now wait a minute, Nate, I . . ."

But Tennet was already moving toward the door, half limping, half staggering.

John Longhurst walked into the kitchen from the outside door, walked to the sink, and levered the pump handle a few times to pull up the ice-cold water in which he washed his hands and face.

His daughter, Julia, came in and said, "Couldn't you have done that at the outside pump?"

He grunted unapologetically, dried his face and hands, and went to the table where the noon meal was spread.

John Longhurst was a man of very few words. His daughter loved him dearly and respected him immensely, and, in this, she was not alone. He had come to this valley when it was empty of humans or cattle. He had built the first house here, the first corral, the first stock pond. But, rather than resist outsiders, he had welcomed newcomers, had moved over to give them room, had helped them in every way at his disposal, sometimes giving a man his first few head of cattle to start his herd. Because of his generosity, Longhurst's ranch was much smaller today than it had once been, but he was not a man who had the need to have more than the next man, or more than a man truly needed. He was wise enough to understand that those things brought no real happiness.

Longhurst had, nonetheless, done well in the cattle business, and his spread was still the largest around. Because he was a simple man whose needs were few, he had plenty of money to share. And he did share. There were few people in the valley who had not been the recipients of his generosity in one way or another.

He was a shy man. He disliked praise and was uncomfortable with compliments. When he saw a need to give money to someone, he usually did so anonymously through someone else. Seldom, however, was anyone in the dark as to the identity of their benefactor. The generosity of John Longhurst was legendary in the valley.

Longhurst was a short man, with broad shoulders and thickly muscled arms and legs. In his younger days, he had been known to be good with his fists and good with a gun. Even now, at fifty-one, no one who knew him mistook his shyness for timidity. He was a man who, without seeking it, received the respect and admiration of those around him, men and women alike.

At thirty years of age, he had won the love of a woman, and she, in turn, had won his. The woman had died young, leaving Longhurst to raise their daughter alone. Now, Julia was a young woman, taller than her father, possessing the physical grace and beauty of her mother.

Longhurst was fiercely protective of Julia, and he worried a good deal about her future. She sometimes felt the need to fight against the constraints his protectiveness placed upon her, but, because she loved him, she suppressed her innate need for independence as much as she was able. And, when she was unable, they quarreled, though Julia could never stay angry with her father for very long, nor he with her.

Despite all his qualities, John Longhurst was not the best company for a young woman who needed to talk and to tell her secrets to someone, and so Julia often rode out to visit friends. The sight of her, mounted on her sorrel mare, was a familiar one on the main roads and side trails of the valley, and her visits were welcomed by nearly everyone. She was as well liked as her father.

She watched him now as he ate, and she asked him, "How was the meeting?"

"Like all meetings. Too much talk, not enough doin'. That Englishman that owns Spade came all the way from England to see his ranch."

"Do you think he's checking up on Derry?"

"Couldn't say. Might be."

"Derry won't like that."

"Derry's got nothin' to say about it. Ain't his ranch."

"And what about the Fergins? Was anything decided?" She waited. Finally, she said, "Well, are you going to tell me?"

"Nope. It ain't women's business. Stay out of it, and let the men handle it."

He purposely avoided looking at her face, knowing how this kind of comment brought her fiery temper to the surface. He continued eating in silence and heard her footsteps as she walked out the door. He knew she would saddle her horse and ride to the home of one of her friends, returning late that evening, and he resigned himself to the fact that he would be eating his supper in the cook shack with the men.

For a while, Nate Tennet fought against the need to rein his horse into the trees alongside the trail and find a spot to camp. The beating he had taken had left him weary in body and soul. It was a long ride to his ranch, and he needed rest. Finally, he decided on a compromise, and, leaving his gelding saddled, he removed its bridle and led it to a small meadow, where he hobbled it and left it.

He knew he would feel better tomorrow. He was young and healthy. He healed quickly. A little rest was all he needed. He threw his blanket down on a bed of fallen needles under a towering pine tree, lowered himself onto it, and was almost instantly asleep.

Once she was out on the trail, feeling the rhythm of the sorrel's easy gait beneath her and smelling the pine scent on the clean air, Julia Longhurst forgot her anger with her father. He was just being protective like always, and she knew that wasn't likely to change any time soon.

She came out of the trees into a small meadow, where she saw a saddled horse grazing. She rode closer and recognized the Cross T brand. Why would a Cross T rider hobble a saddled horse and leave it here, so far from his home range?

She rode in a circle around the meadow and came across the tracks the horse had left coming into the meadow. She followed them.

Nate Tennet, deeply asleep, did not hear Julia approach. She watched him for a few moments, undecided as to what to do. She didn't know how bad off he was, or if he needed help. His face was swollen and bruised. She could clearly see he had taken a bad beating. He had probably felt sick and spread his blanket here, intending to take a brief rest. The sign around his horse, however, showed that the animal had been there for several hours.

Julia rode back out to the meadow, unsaddled Tennet's gelding, and removed the hobbles. She rubbed the animal down with grass and led it to a nearby stream, where she allowed it to drink. She then took it back to the meadow, where she hobbled it again and left it to graze.

Nate Tennet smelled wood smoke and coffee. He fought hard to pull himself out of his sleep, and finally won. He opened his eyes a slit, still feigning sleep, and saw through the blur of his vision someone sitting by the fire. It was a woman. She was sitting on his saddle. He opened his eyes all the way and, feeling sore and stiff in every part of his body, raised himself to a seated position.

The woman smiled at him, and he wondered if he was dreaming. All he could think of to say was, "Is that coffee?"

"Want some?"

He nodded.

She poured a cup and took it over to him.

"Thanks."

"Don't thank me; it's your coffee."

"You got in my saddlebags?"

"Don't worry, I didn't read the letter."

"You'd probably lie about it if you had."

He immediately regretted the comment. She stood up and coldly said, "I'll be on my way."

"Wait, Julia. I'm sorry, I . . . "

She interrupted him. "What is it that makes you want to insult me every time we meet?"

"I'm sorry," he repeated. "I didn't mean it the way it sounded."

She sat down on his saddle again, folded her arms across her breasts, and demanded, "How did you mean it?"

He grinned sheepishly. "I only meant that you would probably not want me to be embarrassed, and would say you hadn't read the letter so as to spare my feelings."

"Now I wish I *had* read it. It must be an interesting letter if it would embarrass you to have me read it."

"Just a correspondence between two friends."

"If it were any of my business, I would have a comment about the friend part. I remember seeing you kiss her in a more-than-friendly way."

Following these words, there was an uncomfortable silence, which Julia broke by pointing to Tennet's face and saying, "You need to get some salve on those cuts."

He reached up, touched his face, and said, "Lazy 8."

"I figured," she said. "Somebody needs to do something about those Fergins." Her voice softened, and she said, "How bad are you hurt?"

"Nothin' serious."

"Of course not. And if it were, you'd probably lie about it."

"All right. Now we're even. Can we just leave it at that?"

"Do you really feel like we're even, Nate? Because I sure don't."

"Aw, you're not still mad about that . . . that thing I said a few years ago."

"Mad? Not really. Considering the source, it's not worth being mad over. But I haven't forgotten."

"I only meant. . ." He stopped. He seemed to be at a loss for words.

She said, "Please, go on. I'd like to see you try to talk your way out of this one."

"All I said was. . ." Again, he was unable to think of the right words.

"You said I looked like a shovel handle in a dress."

"You sure that's what I said?"

She gave him a look that made him self-consciously avert his gaze, and said, "I'll be going now. Your horse has been watered."

"Thanks," he mumbled.

She went to her horse and stepped into the saddle. Tennet pulled himself to his feet, walked over to her, and said, "Listen, I can't help it that you were a skinny kid."

"Your mouth is what you can't help." She spurred away.

"You sure don't look like that anymore," he said in a low voice, as she disappeared into the trees. He knew she hadn't heard him, and he wondered if he maybe should have said it louder. Or would she have been offended by that, too? He admitted to himself that he just didn't understand women.

CHAPTER 4

Dale Ramsey dismounted and wordlessly handed his reins to the hostler. He walked to the main house at Lazy 8 headquarters and knocked on the door.

"Come in."

Ramsey walked in and closed the door behind him. The front room of the house was more of a show place than a place for people to sit and converse. Lorna had decorated it and arranged it to her liking, and she never allowed anyone on the ranch to use it. It was reserved for special guests. Ramsey knew that these special guests were people whom Lorna was trying to impress. One of them was the doctor, who came regularly to attend Saul Fergin.

Ramsey went into an adjoining room through a door that was always closed when any of the special guests came to the house. There, he took a seat in an uncomfortable, dust-covered chair. This room was never cleaned or dusted. Its furnishings consisted of a few mismatched chairs and a desk, behind which sat a woman of about thirty years of age. She had brownish-blonde hair and a well-rounded figure. And she possessed a pair of penetrating brown eyes that had always made Ramsey uneasy. He knew that when she wanted to, Lorna could charm the fangs off a snake, but at this moment, there was nothing charming about her. Nor was there any kindness to be seen in her face, and Ramsey knew one could search in vain for the smallest amount of warmth in the woman's soul. She was a person who cared for money and her own comfort and little else.

She said, "You're late getting back."

"He was late gettin' to town."

"But he got there."

"He got there, and we did it." Said Ramsey.

"And, what?"

"Well, since you ask, I don't like it."

She gazed at Ramsey for a moment, as if trying to bore holes through him with her eyes, and then said, "You don't like what?"

"Don't like handlin' things that way."

"What way?"

"You know what I'm talkin' about, Lorna."

"And you don't like it," she repeated.

Ramsey said nothing. He hated these meetings with Lorna. Hated the woman's sarcasm and her condescending air.

"Do you like your pay?" asked Lorna.

Ramsey gave a grudging nod.

"That pay is what I give you every month to do as you're told whether you like it or not." She waited for her point to settle on Ramsey's mind, and said, "I know you don't like this job, Dale. Your problem is that I pay you more than you could make anywhere else— a lot more—and you hate me for it. You hate me because it keeps you here. I also know that you hate working for a woman." She paused and studied the foreman's face for a few moments, then she said, "Dale, a man can do something he likes to do and make a little money, but in order to make a lot of money, he has to do things he hates. Just keep that in mind, my friend."

Ramsey said nothing. His face was expressionless as he sat there meeting Lorna's gaze. Finally, having made her point, Lorna looked down at the papers before her on the desk,

and said, "How bad did you hurt him?"

"He'll live. He'll ride back home in a day or two."

Lorna Fergin generally showed approval by the absence of any display of disapproval. She did so now. "Did you tell him it was just a warning?"

"Of course I did."

"And does he understand what will happen if he crosses me again?"

Ramsey nodded.

"All right, then. He's been warned. Next time, you know what to do."

Ramsey nodded. Then, changing the subject, he asked, "How's Saul?"

She waved a hand as if to say the topic was of little importance to her. "Saul's dying. You know that. How do you think he is?"

It was her way, thought Ramsey, to make a man feel foolish for having asked a polite question. After a length of silence, Ramsey perceived the meeting was over and said, "Hungry." He stood and left the house.

Walking to the cook shack, he had a moment of self-loathing for doing what he was doing. A self-respecting man should not even work for an outfit like Lazy 8 and associate with the kind of trash the Fergins hired, much less be its foreman and do the bidding of a woman like Lorna.

But Ramsey knew she was right about him. She understood him very well. He would continue doing whatever she asked of him because she paid him more money than he could possibly make anywhere else. How far, he asked himself, would he go for that money? What would he do? How many men would he kill on her orders?

Jack Stull's horse was dead. It was an old horse, and Stull had not taken good care of it. He had ridden it hard, fed it poorly, and beaten it frequently. And now it was dead, and Stull was riding the rails. He had made enemies in the last town and, not having a horse, had narrowly escaped their retribution, bringing nothing with him but the clothes he wore.

He climbed into an open boxcar in a train yard in the middle of a cold night, and in the darkness found a corner where he planned to get some sleep. His boot stepped on something that moved, and an angry voice cried out, "Hey, watch where you're steppin'."

Jack Stull thumbed a match alight and saw a man wrapped in blankets. The man looked old and used up. His face was an unpleasant combination of gray stubble whiskers, wrinkles, and mottled red-and-purple-toned flesh. His eyes were rheumy and red-rimmed. He uttered a string of curses and barked, "Put out that match. What I gotta do to get you to leave a man alone so he can get some sleep?"

Stull was about to say something when the car lurched as the train started to move. He found an empty corner and sat in it, leaning back against the cold wood of the boxcar's wall. The old man continued cursing him for a moment in a raspy voice, and then rolled back into his blankets and was silent.

The train reached its full speed, and the car rocked from side to side on the tracks, its iron wheels clicking below. It made Stull sleepy, but he was cold—had been cold for hours—and he knew he would not sleep tonight because of it. He had tried to pull the door shut when he entered the car, but it was stuck, leaving a three-foot opening through which the frigid night air came into the boxcar.

Stull thought of the old man in the corner, wrapped in blankets. He rose and walked over to where the old man lay, struck another match, and said, "Where'd you get them blankets?"

The old man stirred and, after a stream of impassioned cursing, said, "The brakeman gives 'em out, along with cream pies and hot cider, just for ridin' his train." He followed this with another burst of profanity and said, "What's it matter where I got 'em. They're mine. Now leave me be."

If there had been more light in the car, if the old man had been able to see Stull's smile, he would have probably been afraid. As it was, he merely cursed a few more times and fell silent again.

Stull went back to his corner and waited, listening to the sound of the wheels below him, listening for a certain tone. When it came, when the tracks gave off the hollow sound from a wooden trestle, he sprang to his feet, ran over, pulled the blankets off the old man, and jerked him to his feet.

The old man gave a bellow of indignation as he was pulled across the car toward the door. When he realized what was happening, he screeched in terror and began struggling with all his strength. But, he was old and thin, and Stull was a big man. Stull thrust the old man into the opening, and the old man caught the edge of the door and clung to it with both hands. Stull hit him hard with a burly shoulder, but the old man hung on stubbornly.

Leaning back, Stull raised a booted foot and gave the old man a powerful kick in the chest, breaking his grip and hurling him out of the car. The old man hit the edge of the trestle, bounced, and flew out into open space and then down, down, down—to the bottom of the canyon.

Laughing with malicious pleasure, Stull wrestled with the door, finally managing to close it. He crossed to the corner where the old man's blankets lay in disarray, straightened them, and rolled himself into them.

They were still warm.

Nate Tennet stayed for two days at the Cross T, the ranch where he had up until recently been foreman. The Lanes, the older couple who owned the ranch, were close friends of his, and it was Mrs. Lane who insisted he stay longer after he told her he only intended to stay overnight.

She said, "It won't hurt you to let somebody take care of you for a couple of days. Nobody will accuse you of acting the baby. Anyway, what you need most is some of my cooking. I can imagine how you men eat at your place: fried bacon, fried bread, fried potatoes, and never a green in sight."

On the day he left, she hugged him and gave him a sack filled with fresh vegetables from her garden. "They're greens," she said. "You eat them."

As Tennet rode toward his house, which he had built himself, he saw that his barn was no longer standing. It had been burned to the ground. It must have happened the previous night, because smoke was still issuing from the ashes. The tack shed had also been burned, the gate was open, and there were cattle all around the yard. The door of the house was open, and a fat steer was just coming out. Tennet knew instantly what had happened, and anger boiled within him. He tied his horse and went inside. He chased out another steer and surveyed the damage.

The place had been wrecked before the cattle had been allowed in. The cupboards had been torn from the walls and smashed, the windows had been broken, the mattress on his bed had been slashed and its stuffing pulled out. His possessions were all scattered and smashed on the floor. Pieces of hay were everywhere, and Tennet knew someone had thrown a few pitchforks of it into the house to attract cattle. A few of the floorboards were broken from the weight of the steers that had roamed around inside. There was very little left that was worth keeping. Tennet was glad his hired hands hadn't been there. They might have been killed. Fortunately, they were out working in the haying.

He went back outside and walked over to survey the ashes of his barn. He knew this had been brought on—like the beating he had received—by his interest in a piece of land called Yellowbush Flat. Lorna Fergin wanted it, too—apparently very badly. She claimed she wanted it for the grass, but Tennet was unconvinced. Something told him there was more to it than that. But, what?

Yellowbush Flat was government land and would be going up for auction soon. Lorna Fergin had sent her foreman, Dale Ramsey, to warn Tennet not to bid on the land—or else. But, Tennet had ignored the warning and placed his name on the list of interested parties. And now Lorna Fergin was sending him a clear message not to defy her. Tennet didn't know Lorna very well, but he was sure she was not a person who gave up easily. He didn't know what to expect next, but he knew he would need to be alert.

He pondered the situation and shook his head at the irony. What Lorna Fergin didn't know was that if she, as his neighbor, had come to him and told him she wished to purchase Yellowbush Flat, and asked him as a favor not to bid on it, Tennet would have graciously acceded to her polite request—it was a decent piece of graze, but it wasn't anything he couldn't do without. But when she sent her emissary to warn him off and threaten him, she virtually guaranteed that Tennet would fight her tooth and nail.

"Maybe I'm not the only one that doesn't understand the way some folks think," he said aloud to himself.

It was nearly dark when the train stopped in a small town, and Jack Stull, having seen the sign announcing the town's name, climbed out of the boxcar, carrying the rolled-up blankets that had only recently been the property of an old man, now deceased.

Stull walked to the nearest saloon and, leaving the blanket roll outside, went in and walked up to the bar. Catching the attention of the bartender, he asked the name of the owner of the saloon.

"Simmons. Who wants to know?"

"So it's Simmons, is it? Happens he's an old friend of mine."

The bartender's face showed skepticism. Stull looked like a man who didn't have two nickels to rub together. The bartender said, "He ain't here right now."

"When do you expect him back?"

"Tomorrow."

Stull nodded. "I'll come back then. He'll be mighty glad to see me." He started to walk away, then turned and casually took two sandwiches from the free lunch platter, quickly making his exit. He didn't know anyone named Simmons.

He found a secluded spot behind one of the buildings opposite the saloon and sat with his back against a wall, eating the sandwiches. As he ate, he contemplated his fortunes. Because of the long train ride he had just completed, he was a good deal closer to his destination, but now he needed a horse and saddle. After eating, he went into a different saloon, and there inquired as to the location of the Lazy 8 ranch. He was told it was a good three-hour ride on horseback, and he was given the name of the nearest town.

The thought of walking there never crossed Jack Stull's mind. He avoided it whenever he could. He thought about stealing a horse, but rejected the idea. Instead, he went down the street to the telegraph office and said to the operator, "I need to send a telegram."

The operator eyed him with a mixture of caution and suspicion, and pushed a pad of paper and a pencil across the counter. Stull wrote his brief message and slid the paper back across. The telegrapher looked at the message and then looked up, "You'll need to pay in advance."

Stull said, "I'll have to pay later—when they come and get me."

The telegrapher started to say something, but Stull looked at him with eyes that the man would later tell his wife were "pure, two hundred-proof evil," and said, "Mister, I don't plan to argue with you. You'll get your money. Now, send that message."

The message arrived at the Lazy 8 ranch the following morning. Lorna Fergin read it and scowled. How had he found her? She sat down at her desk and spent a good ten minutes in silent contemplation. Finally, she went out to the yard and called one of the Mexican horse wranglers over, and gave him very specific instructions, along with a detailed description of Jack Stull. "Bring him here," she said. "But don't talk to him. Pretend like you don't speak English. Can you do that?"

The wrangler nodded.

CHAPTER 5

The Rupp farm had never been a very prosperous place; Old Todd Rupp had always spent more time drinking than working. But as Kyle Rupp, Todd's oldest son, got his first look at the farm in over two years, he realized he had never seen the place looking this run down. In spite of this, he felt a real sense of excitement at coming home. He felt the thrill of seeing familiar things he had missed. Kyle had spent the last two years working for a mining company in Colorado, driving an ore wagon. A job his uncle had procured for him. He was now nineteen years old.

His younger brother, Willie, was out in the yard, ineffectually trying to stop the chickens from getting into the granary, unable, as usual, to figure out a plan for accomplishing a simple task. Willie had been like that his whole life. He had been born that way.

Kyle rode into the yard, and Willie turned quickly, fear on his face. It took only a second for the boy's face to show recognition, and for his troubled expression to transform into a huge smile. He shouted Kyle's name and ran to him.

Kyle swung out of the saddle and received his younger brother's embrace, remembering how it had always embarrassed him in the past to have people see these demonstrations of Willie's affection. Now, he didn't care who saw it. He was home, and he had missed the kid.

There was, however, no one around to witness the homecoming. They were alone. Kyle had his look around the homestead, including a stop to visit the graves of his and Willie's parents. Their mother's grave was now over ten years old, but their father's was still fresh. Kyle thought it was odd that there was no marker on his father's grave, but he said nothing about it to Willie. "Where is everybody, Willie? Where's Dax and Rudy?" he asked.

"Pa died."

"I know that. I got a letter from Mrs. Lane. But, where's Dax and Rudy?"

"Rudy got killed, and Dax just left after that."

"Rudy got killed? How?"

"Don't know. He went to town, and then he didn't come back. Dax said he must've got drunk, but the next morning, he was layin' out on the bridge. Dax said somebody shot him."

"Who?"

"He said it was Lazy 8."

"Why would Mr. Fergin's crew do that? We never did anything to them."

Willie shook his head, and Kyle knew the boy had no more information to offer.

Suddenly, Willie let out a cry and ran to the granary and started chasing hens away from the door. Some of them ran inside. Willie ran around, scattering dust and hens, making no real progress, growing increasingly frustrated.

Kyle walked over and took Willie's hand. "Here's how you do it," he said patiently. "You go inside the granary and chase all the hens outside, then you close the door so they can't get back in."

Kyle demonstrated the operation and allowed Willie to close the door and put the nail through the hasp to keep it closed. Willie laughed as he did so, freed from a worrisome problem. Kyle knew his brother was glad to have him back.

Together, they crossed the yard and went up the steps to the porch and through the front door. Kyle was appalled at the state of the interior of the house. "How long ago did Dax leave?" he asked. Looking around, he realized it must have been several weeks at the least.

"Day before yesterday."

Kyle nodded. He had known that would be Willie's answer. The boy had no notion of time, and any time before the day he was in was, to him, the day before yesterday. Kyle felt his heart swell with love for Willie, his only sibling, and now his only remaining family, and as he surveyed the conditions in which the boy had been living, it almost made him weep.

"What have you been eating?" he asked.

"Oats and eggs."

"Do you cook them?"

"I eat 'em the way we did when we ran away."

When Kyle had been just a boy, on an occasion when he had become angry with their drunken father, he had decided to run away. Willie had begged to go with him, and Kyle had never been able to say no to his little brother. They gathered some eggs, put some oats in a sack, and poured some milk in a mason jar. They rolled these items in a blanket, and headed out on their ponies with no particular destination in mind.

It didn't take Kyle long to realize they had overlooked a long list of things they would need on the trail, including cooking equipment and eating utensils. Soon, impelled by their hunger, they began eating the oats straight out of the bag, washing them down with milk. And Kyle taught Willie how to poke a hole in one end of an egg shell and suck out the egg. Like most children who run away, the two boys soon decided they liked their home better than they had previously thought and turned their ponies around.

Now, looking around the kitchen, Kyle saw the floor and table were littered with eggshells and oats. The milk pail was sitting next to the back door, half full of milk. He checked it and found the milk to be curdled, and he wondered why. Milking was one thing Willie could do right. The boy had been milking the family cow for years. She was a docile animal, and she knew when milking time was. She would walk to the customary place in the corral and stand patiently until her udder was emptied. There was no need of a halter or kick chain; she was perfectly cooperative.

Willie also understood that animals needed to be fed twice a day, and that humans didn't eat until the animals were taken care of. Kyle was grateful for this. The animals appeared to have been eating better than Willie had.

Worried now, Kyle said, "Have you been milking the cow?"

"Cow's gone."

"Where to?"

"Mr. Pocker." Willie had never been able to correctly pronounce the name Proctor.

"What's Mr. Proctor doing with our cow?" asked Kyle.

"I sold her to him."

Kyle's head dropped onto his chest. He remained thus for a moment, and then he looked at his brother and said, "How much did he give you?" Kyle knew about the Proctors. They were a slovenly outfit that had a farm west of town. He had never liked or trusted Carl Proctor, and he hoped the man hadn't taken too much advantage of Willie. He asked, "How much did he give you?"

Willie went to the cupboard and took out a jar. He handed it to Kyle. It held a few coins, which totaled exactly one dollar.

"Is this all of it?" Kyle asked, already knowing there would have been no opportunity for Willie to spend any of it.

"Yes," said Willie, proudly.

Kyle made no comment. There was no point in making Willie feel bad about what he had done. He said, "Bring the broom, Willie, and we'll do a little cleaning. Then I'm going to cook us some ham and eggs."

Willie's eyes grew large, and Kyle could imagine how much the boy had missed good food.

It took two hours to clean the house. Willie worked just as hard as Kyle, though he had to be told everything to do. Afterward, Kyle sent the boy out to gather eggs while he cut some slices off a ham he had found hanging in the smokehouse.

While they were eating, something occurred to Kyle. He had not seen any graves on the premises except for those of his parents. He said, "Where is Rudy buried?"

"Under the bridge."

Kyle stopped chewing, "You buried him by yourself, didn't you?"

Willie gave a proud nod of his head. "Just me alone."

Kyle knew that no one else would have buried a body in the soft gravel of the creek bed under the bridge. But Willie was waiting for his praise, and Kyle gave it to him. "Looks like you're pretty good at runnin' things by yourself."

The comment had the opposite of its intended effect. Willie's face clouded up with genuine terror, his eyes filled with tears, and he said, "You ain't leavin' me alone again, are you, Kyle?"

"No," said Kyle, quickly. "Not ever, Willie. I'll never leave you alone again. Remember when we ran away? I was goin' alone, but you begged me not to leave you, so I took you."

Mollified, Willie smiled and resumed eating, wolfing his food like the half-starved boy he was. And Kyle had a better understanding of how bad it must have been for his brother to be on his own for the first time in his life. Dax must have left in a big hurry, he thought.

24

The man had not even taken time to bury the body of his long-time friend, Rudy, or inform neighbors of Willie's circumstances.

After eating, Kyle went out to the bridge and slid down the steep bank to the dry creek bed. He found Rudy's grave and what was left of Rudy's scattered remains. The shallow covering of sand and fine gravel Willie had thrown on the body had been no deterrent to coyotes and other scavengers.

Kyle didn't want Willie to see this. Knowing what he would find here, he had given the boy some work to do while he came to investigate. He would wait for Willie to go to sleep tonight, and come back out, gather up the remains, and bury them behind the house, where his parents were buried. Rudy deserved that much.

He was turning to leave when something caught his eye. It was a wooden grave marker, lying facedown on the gravel of the creek bed. He walked to it and turned it over. The marker had been well crafted—obviously not by Willie. Someone, probably Rudy or Dax— had taken some time to cut the plank and artistically carve the words and dates in it. Immediately, Kyle saw that it was his father's marker. Willie must have taken it from his father's grave and brought it out here to mark Rudy's resting place.

A smile began to form on Kyle's face as he thought of his brother's innocent goodness, but it disappeared when he read the writing carved below his father's name.

Murdered by the Lazy 8

Mrs. Lane had not said in her letter that Todd Rupp had been murdered; she had simply written that he had died, omitting to mention the cause. What had happened in this valley? Saul Fergin had often bought hay from the Rupps. Kyle would not have called Fergin a friend, but he could see no reason why he would want to do harm to a local farmer and his hired hand.

Something had changed around here, and Kyle decided he'd better find out what it was.

When Jack Stull arrived at Lazy 8 headquarters, he was weary from his long trip, but extremely interested in this situation Priscilla had managed to worm her way into. The driver who had picked him up had refused to answer any questions or even talk to him, and Stull knew that was on orders from Priscilla.

He went inside the house without knocking, and was looking around the front room when Priscilla entered. They stood looking at each other for a few moments, and finally, Stull said, "Kind of run out on me, didn't you, Sis?"

She snorted. "I have no obligation to you. I'll go where I want without your permission."

"And I'll always find you."

"Apparently so," she said, resignation in her voice. "So how *did* you find me?"

"Ran into an old friend. Nestor Bradley."

Priscilla's face went white, and Stull laughed. "Figured that would get your attention." He laughed again and said, "I was admirin' the ranch as we drove in. Big place. Lot of land. I'd ask how you come to own it, but I can pretty much guess. You married an old man, and not long after the weddin', he started feelin' sickly. Doctor couldn't do much for him, and despite all your tender ministrations, he died, leavin' you with a broken heart, along with his ranch and all his money. Does that sound like the story, Priscilla dear?"

Priscilla looked furtively around, acting almost panicked. "Keep your voice down," she said in a loud whisper. She motioned him to follow her to her office, and closed the door behind them.

Stull looked around the filthy room and said, "Nice place. Ma would be proud of your house-keepin' habits."

"If you don't like it, clean it yourself. I've got more important things on my mind than sweeping floors." Then she said, "What do you want from me, Jack?"

"First, I want an answer, Pris."

The urgency returned to her voice. "Don't call me Priscilla. I'm Lorna around here. Now, tell me what you want from me."

"First tell me: Did I get the story right?"

She clenched her jaws for a moment, clearly angry and undecided about what to do. Finally, she said, "Close. He isn't dead."

"Oh. He isn't dead. Well in that case, I'd like to meet him. After all, he's my brother-in-law."

"You can't."

"Don't tell me, Sis. He's poorly. He took sick not long after he married you, am I right?"

With obvious reluctance, she nodded. Then, talking over his gloating laugh, she said, "It's not like you think, Jack. He's got a lot of debts. He hasn't managed his business affairs well, and when he dies, I'll be left owing a lot of money."

Smiling in incredulity, Stull said, "Don't lie to me, Sis. You'd never get yourself into a situation like that. You'd find out everything there was to know about him before gettin' hitched to him."

Again, she asked, "What do you want?"

"Half."

"Half his debts? I'll be happy to give you all of them."

"Let's not play games, Pris. . . Lorna. You wouldn't be here if there wasn't somethin' big in it for you. Anyhow, Nestor Bradley already told me it has somethin' to do with a railroad."

Priscilla picked up a paperweight and slammed it down on the desk. "Bradley's got a big mouth."

"Only when he's drunk."

"He quit drinking three years ago."

"He gave in to temptation. A man can only stay dry for so long."

"You got him drunk?"

Stull shrugged, sat down in a chair, and said, "Wasn't hard to convince him that one little drink wouldn't hurt anything. He took it from there."

Priscilla's shoulders slumped in resignation. "I won't give you half. I've worked too hard to set this all up."

"I can negotiate a little, but not much."

"One-fourth," she said, in a flat tone.

"I can't negotiate that far."

"You'll have to. That's all you're getting."

"I could go to the sheriff."

"And he'd arrest you first, before he came to get me."

"I could send him a note."

"Come on, Jack. You said you didn't want to play games."

"All right. One-third."

"I'll give you a third of what I get out of this ranch when I sell it, but nothing else. I've got some other deals I'm working on; you get none of that. That's final."

"All right," said Stull, and they shook hands.

Stull said, "I'll need some front money."

"What for?"

"I need clothes, a horse, and a saddle, for starters.

27

"You can have my husband's horse and saddle." She gave a wicked smile. "He won't be needing them again. I'll give you some of his clothes, too."

Stull smiled with her, and an onlooker, if there had been any, would have been able to observe a family resemblance between the two.

Stull said, "That's fine, but I want some spendin' money, too."

"You mean gambling money."

Stull's face closed up, and the churlish look it took on was as familiar to Priscilla as it was unpleasant, reminding her just how much she hated him. Stull said, "It's my business how I spend my money."

"And it's my business how you spend *my* money."

"You've got plenty, Sis. Don't think I don't know about your bank account in Chicago."

Priscilla was pensive for a moment, and then, as if having come to a decision, she said, "I've spent it all on this deal."

"What do you mean?"

"Nestor Bradley and I have it all arranged. He told me where the railroad spur is going, and I've bought all the land I could along the route. The railroad will pay me a lot of money for the right-of-way across all the land I own. Even after I split it with Bradley, it will be enough for me to retire on."

He smiled skeptically. "There ain't enough money in the world for you, Sis. You'll never retire."

Priscilla scowled, but said nothing.

Stull looked around the room and said, "Where's the picture?"

"What picture?"

"You know the one I mean. The one Gladys hated so much."

"You mean the portrait?"

Stull rolled his eyes. "All right. The portrait. "Where is it?"

A faint, smile of malice came onto Priscilla's lips. "It's with her."

"What do you mean, it's with her? She's dead."

"It's hanging on the wall of her mausoleum."

Stull threw back his head and laughed. Priscilla smiled and there was a certain amount of pride in her smile.

Stull said, "I've been wonderin' about the way the old lady died. Folks told me the doctors never could figure out what she had."

Priscilla's expression was bland, "Are you planning on trying to use that one against me?"

"Not as long as I get my third of this deal. After that we'll have to have another talk about our partnership."

"Partnership? No, Jack. We're not partners. You'll get a third of this one and then we'll part ways."

Stull just smiled, and Priscilla knew that smile signified trouble for her.

That night, Priscilla lay in her bed in the room next to where her dying husband lay, his stertorous breathing reaching into her room. She had considered moving to a room on the other side of the house, where she would not be bothered by the sounds of the man's suffering, but had decided against it. It wouldn't look right. People needed to see her as a loving, concerned wife.

As she lay there, she contemplated this most recent turn of events. She had not expected Jack to find her, had hoped never to see him again. But as long as he was here, perhaps he could be useful to her. She was concerned about her foreman, Dale Ramsey. He was corrupt, but he had that strange, hypocritical sense of honor she had often seen in men, particularly these western men. He would need watching. Briefly, she considered replacing him with Jack, but she immediately discarded the notion. Jack did not know how to manage men. If he were made foremen, half the crew would quit the first week, and in a month's time, the bunkhouse would be virtually empty.

Men hated Jack, and Priscilla understood that—*she* hated Jack. She had hated him since her childhood. However, if it came to killing—and it probably would—Jack could prove very useful.

CHAPTER 6

The day after arriving home, Kyle Rupp rode over to the Cross T. He took Willie with him, because Willie was terrified of being left alone again. The Cross T was one of the larger ranches in the area. Ezra Lane and his wife, Leah, had come to the valley with their four daughters shortly after John Longhurst had arrived, and had begun building their herd from cows given to them by Longhurst. They were a kind-hearted people, and they and their daughters were well regarded in the valley.

They had hired Nate Tennet as a regular puncher when he was sixteen years old, and he had become their foreman at the age of twenty. The Lanes had had only daughters—seven of them—and Nate had come to be like the son they had never had. The daughters were all married now, and Nate was building his own spread, but the kindly old couple still looked upon him as though he were family.

Kyle and Willie were well received at the Cross T, and Mrs. Lane fed them before even allowing Kyle to state his business. Neither of the two boys resisted; they were already getting tired of ham and eggs.

After eating, Kyle said, "Mrs. Lane, can you tell me what's been happening around here? It appears that my father and one of our hands were killed by the Lazy 8."

Mrs. Lane's eyebrows went up. "Which of your hands? Dax or Rudy?"

"Rudy. Willie says Dax took off right after Rudy was killed."

"I didn't know about that. Who's been taking care of Willie?"

"Nobody."

Her eyes widened. "He's been alone?"

"Yes."

"For how long?"

Kyle sent her a signal with his eyes and almost imperceptibly angled his head toward Willie.

Mrs. Lane caught on immediately and said, "Willie, would you go out back and bring me an armload of firewood?"

When the boy was gone, Kyle told Mrs. Lane about the burying of Rudy's body in the creek bed, and the state of the remains when he had found them. He said, "Hard to tell, but I'd say he'd been dead for around a month."

Her hand went to her mouth. "Oh. Poor little Willie. How did he survive? What did he eat? No wonder he looks so skinny."

Kyle told her all he could about Willie's solitary ordeal, and asked, "Why would Mr. Fergin want to attack us?"

Her expression grew hard. "Not Mr. Fergin. The ranch is now being run by Mrs. Fergin, his wife."

"He's married?"

"Yes, and she's purely evil if you ask me."

"Why is she running the ranch?"

"Saul took sick a few months after the wedding."

There was a brief silence as she and Kyle exchanged a significant look. Then, Mrs. Lane resumed talking. "Lorna—that's her name—seems to want more land. But it's specific pieces of land that she's after."

"Is that what she's killing people for?" asked Kyle.

"I can't say. To my knowledge, it's never been proven that the Lazy 8 killed your father. Sheriff Benson investigated, and couldn't find any evidence. But if someone were to come up with proof that Lorna Fergin was behind his and Rudy's killings, it wouldn't be a big surprise to anybody around here."

"But why? Why were they killed?"

"That, I don't know. There must be a reason, though." She was pensive for a moment, and she said, "I can tell you that Lorna wants Yellowbush Flat. She wants it badly enough to warn Nate Tennet not to bid on it when it goes up for auction, and to have her men give him a pretty bad beating when he defied her. They pretty much let him know that if he crosses them again, they'll kill him."

There was another silence, and Mrs. Lane said, "You could be in danger too, you know. If anyone from the Lazy 8 asks, you'd better tell them you aren't interested in Yellowbush Flat."

Kyle was having these same thoughts, and to hear someone else say them caused a chill to go through him. He pondered the situation for a moment and asked her for a pencil and piece of paper, and then, sitting on the opposite side of the table from her, he drew a crude map of the valley, roughly outlining the borders of the different ranches. Next, he penciled in the position of Yellowbush Flat. It was the piece of land that separated his father's farm from Nate Tennet's ranch.

Kyle said, "Pa always coveted that piece of land. If it had come up for auction, he would have bid on it. There's no doubt."

"But why would Lorna Fergin want it so badly?" said Mrs. Lane. "It's a nice piece of land for farming, but there's nothing special about it from a rancher's point of view."

"Nothing that we can see," observed Kyle. "Maybe there's gold on it or something like that."

She shook her head. "I doubt it. There's never been anyone prospecting on it. The creek flows across one corner of it, but that creek crosses the entire range. We all get water from it and the other creeks, too. We don't need to go to Yellowbush Flat for that." There was a silence, and Mrs. Lane said, "Maybe it's the railroad."

"What do you mean?"

"You've been gone," she said. "There's a lot of talk about building a spur from the main line north for nearly a hundred miles. There are a lot of towns and ranches along that stretch. There's money to be made shipping cattle, and there's some logging starting up north of here, and even some mining. There were some surveyors looking around about six months ago, but they weren't saying much. What if . . . ?"

Kyle interrupted her. Looking down at his hand-drawn map, he said, "Yellowbush Flat would be the perfect place for the tracks to come through. They could come up over that little saddle and miss the higher ridges. Because of the mountains, there's no place as good for miles in either direction."

Mrs. Lane's eyes shone with excitement. "And whoever owns it could make a lot of money." After a moment, she sobered. She looked at Kyle, compassion in her eyes. "Your father must have refused to promise he wouldn't bid on Yellowbush Flat, so they killed him."

Remembering the inscription on his father's grave marker, *Murdered by Lazy 8,* Kyle thought of how Carl Proctor had taken advantage of Willie and paid only a dollar for the milk cow. He said,

"Rudy and Dax were probably trying to protect the farm for me and Willie. They must have stood up to Lazy 8."

"And," she supplied, "Rudy was killed, and Dax knew he would be next if he didn't hightail it."

Kyle frowned. "That brings up another question: Why didn't Lazy 8 kill Nate Tennet like they killed my father and Rudy?"

Mrs. Lane acted uncomfortable. "I think I know. Nate is a rancher, and he's well liked in the valley . . ."

Kyle interrupted, "And my father was neither."

"I'm sorry, Kyle. Things aren't always the way they should be."

"It's all right, Mrs. Lane. I grew up knowing my father was a drunk. He had a fine piece of land, but he didn't work hard enough to make anything fine out of it. And added to that, he was a farmer, and this is ranching country. I doubt very many people even took much notice when he was killed. But if something bad happens to a rancher around here, everybody takes notice."

She nodded her head sympathetically, and for a moment tried to think of something to say. But there was nothing.

Nate Tennet was nowhere to be seen when Kyle Rupp rode up to the house, having left Willie in the care of Mrs. Lane. Nate stepped out from behind a tree, holding a rifle. Recognizing Kyle, he smiled and lowered the weapon. "Hello, Kyle. Didn't know you were back. Heard about your father. Sorry."

"They killed Rudy too."

"I didn't know that."

"Nobody did, except for Dax and Willie and the people that did it."

"When'd it happen?"

"Don't know for sure. Maybe three or four weeks ago." He looked at the pile of ash that had been Tennet's barn and shook his head solemnly.

Tennet said, "Get down and come in. It's a mess, but I could make some coffee."

Inside the house, there were piles of debris that Tennet had swept up. He was in the process of cleaning up the mess, but it still looked like the aftermath of a stampede.

Kyle said, "Lazy 8 do all this?"

"Who else would?"

"Yeah."

They talked for a while, and Kyle pulled out the map he had drawn. He unfolded it, laying it on a clean spot on the floor, and told Tennet what he and Mrs. Lane had deduced about the situation.

Standing above Kyle, looking down at the map, Tennet said, "It makes sense. You might be right." Then he bent down and said, "Wait a minute. There's something you missed." He pointed at a spot on the map. "Right here there's a ridge. The tracks would have to make a bend to go around it, and that would mean they would cross your father's farm. Maybe your pa refused to sell his farm to Lorna Fergin. Maybe that's why they killed him."

For several long minutes, neither of them spoke as they solemnly gazed at the map. Finally, Tennet said, "Bring that paper outside."

Kyle picked up the map, and they both went outside, where Tennet took the map and laid it on the ground, using small rocks as paperweights. With a stick, he began tracing lines in the dirt around the map. He said, "We need to look at the whole picture. Now, look, here's the town, and here's my ranch, your farm, Yellowbush Flat."

Tennet squatted there, pensively rubbing his chin, unconsciously avoiding places that were still sore or scabbed over from the beating he had taken. All at once, he brightened and said, "I've got it. It's as clear as a bell."

Kyle watched in fascination as Tennet outlined what he was sure was Lorna Fergin's plan.

"You can't just bypass a town with the rails," explained Tennet, "unless it's just too small to matter. But you can't always find a way to go right into the town, either. Some depots are a mile or more from the town they serve. That doesn't matter much, as long as there's a good road between the town and the depot.

"You can see that the ridges and mountains all along here, on both sides, would make it impractical to run the tracks into town. They would run across Yellowbush Flat and your father's farm, and right here would be the depot."

"In our hay field?"

"Exactly."

"But what good would a depot be if there's no road into town?"

"Somebody would have to build the road." Using the stick, Tennet drew a line that ran from the Rupp's hayfield, eastward straight across an open area to the square he had drawn in the dirt that represented the town.

Kyle nodded. "You've got to be right. That's why Lorna Fergin wanted Pa's farm."

"Do you see the other part too?

Kyle smiled an ironic smile. "Yeah. The other part of the road—after it leaves Pa's hayfield—cuts right across the Lazy 8."

Tennet nodded. "And if Lorna Fergin gets your land and Yellowbush Flat, she'll own the whole stretch, from the railroad to town. And it's a sure bet she won't let anyone besides herself build a road across her land."

"What would happen to the town if there was no road?"

"There's no two ways to answer that one," said Tennet soberly. "The town that gets bypassed by the railroad dies."

Silently they walked together into the house, silently Tennet made the coffee, and silently they sipped it, until Tennet said, "Lorna will be after us both, you know. I've been careful, and I think she's been afraid to kill me, but I know the time's coming when she'll have to send someone after me." He looked directly at Kyle and said, "Unless you're willing to give your land away, you may need to leave this valley as soon as you can."

Kyle said, "I've got nowhere to go. I've got the farm; there's nothing else. It's where Willie and I have lived all our lives, and I don't intend to leave it to the likes of Lazy 8."

"They might kill you."

Kyle shrugged his shoulders. He had no answer other than to say, "I'm not leavin'."

It was almost dark when Kyle rode up to the Proctor farm. It looked worse than he remembered it. It occurred to him that his father's farm would look about like this if it hadn't been for him, and the thought gave him a brief moment of satisfaction. From the time he had been able to do so, Kyle had tried to take over the chores and tasks his father had neglected because of his drinking, and by the time he was thirteen years old, Kyle had run the farm, even to the point of supervising the hired hands—men much older than himself.

Things at the farm had gotten a little run down during the two years he had been away, but nothing like what he was seeing at this moment as he surveyed Carl Proctor's place. He hailed the house and waited. Someone stirred the ragged curtains in a window facing him. After too long a time, Carl Proctor casually stepped out onto the porch and grunted an ungracious hello. He was wearing a gun.

"Hello, Mr. Proctor. I need to talk to you," said Kyle.

The only change on Proctor's face was a slight narrowing of the eyes. "Then talk."

"You know what it's about."

"Can't imagine," said Proctor, in a voice that was completely toneless. He was acting bored, Kyle realized. Was it for the purpose of dissembling, or was he truly that uninterested in Kyle's reason for coming here? Kyle pulled a small bag from his pocket and said, "Here's your dollar. I'd like the cow back."

Proctor's face hardened into an insolent smile. "You ain't getting' her back. I bought her fair."

"You knew my brother was alone. You knew my father was dead, the hands were gone, and I was away."

"Yep, I knew all that. And that was what gave your brother the authority to sell that cow. He sold her, and I'm keepin' her."

"You paid a dollar for her."

"That was the price he asked."

Kyle felt his frustration growing inside him. He said, "Willie's not right in the head. You knew that. You took advantage of it."

"Ain't none of my business if he's right in the head or not. He was the only Rupp around, so he was the only one I could deal with."

"We don't have to argue about this. You know what you did was wrong. I'm giving your money back." Kyle tossed the sack of coins on the porch and said, "I'm takin' my cow."

He started to rein the horse around, when Proctor pulled the pistol out of his waistband and said in an icy voice, "I'll kill any man that comes onto my land and tries to steal any of my livestock. A man has a right to defend what's his."

"That's exactly what *I'm* doing," shouted Kyle in impotent anger.

Proctor raised the pistol and said, "Get off my land." He cocked the gun.

Kyle glared at him for a moment, then swung the horse around and spurred him into a run. He ran the brute until he realized he was taking his anger at Proctor out on the horse, then he slowed to a gallop and finally to a walk. He rode the rest of the way home, filled with frustrated outrage.

When Kyle rode into the yard, there was a strange horse tied to the hitching post next to the house. It bore the Lazy 8 brand. Willie was nowhere to be seen, nor was the rider of the horse. Kyle went inside and found a man sitting in the front room, his dusty boots propped up on the table. His hat was on his head, and his head was bowed on his chest, as if he had been dozing.

Kyle was not in the mood for visitors, and the man's effrontery irked him. He said, "Who are you?"

This man raised his head, and his mouth formed a smile that sent a chill through Kyle. The man said, "I'm a friend." His voice held a mocking tone.

Kyle wanted to tell him to leave, but there was such an overpowering aura of danger about this man that he curbed his tongue. He said, "What do you want?"

"I just came to give you and your kid brother a chance to save yourselves a lot of trouble."

"How?"

"By signin' a paper."

Kyle allowed a long silence to pass before he spoke. "Are you running us off our own farm?"

The man stood up and looked squarely at Kyle, his hand near the butt of his pistol. He said, "You heard me. I don't discuss things, and I don't repeat myself. Do you understand what I'm sayin', boy?"

Kyle looked down at the floor and nodded.

The man pulled a folded paper out of his shirt pocket and said, "Sign it."

"No."

The man went around behind the chair where he had been sitting and reached down. He lifted Willie up by an arm, and Kyle could see the fear in Willie's white face. The man pulled his pistol, and Willie began to scream in terror.

"Don't hurt him," Kyle said, speaking over Willie's screams.

The man passed the paper over to Kyle and said, "You got a pen?"

Kyle found a pen and ink and signed the paper. He handed it to the man, who let go of Willie's hand, and Willie collapsed on the floor, still wailing.

The man reached in his pocket and pulled out some scrip. Setting it on the table, he said, "There's a hundred dollars there. You've been paid. You've sold the farm and everything on it, understand?"

Kyle nodded.

The man said, "There's a couple of nags out in the pasture. We don't want 'em. You've got two days to get gone." He walked out.

After the man had ridden away, Kyle lifted Willie and sat in the chair, holding the boy close to him. Presently, Willie stopped crying and said, "Is he gone?"

Kyle nodded.

Willie's eyes filled with tears again. "He's makin' us leave, ain't he?"

Kyle said, "We'll find a better place," but in his heart, he didn't believe the words. There were undoubtedly many places in the world better than their little farm, but this was home. It was the only home either of them had ever known. Moreover, it was theirs. Their father had done that one thing for his sons; he had left them a farm that was free of financial encumbrance.

"What are we?" he said aloud. "Are we nothing? A man comes in and steals our only milk cow, and then pulls a gun on me when I ask for it back. Another man comes in and orders us off our own land."

Gently, he pushed Willie away from him. He went to his father's room. Everything there seemed untouched, and probably had been since the day of his father's death. He opened a drawer and found the pistol his father had always kept there. He took it out, checked the loads, and shoved it into his belt. He found two boxes of cartridges in the drawer and took those too. He turned to Willie and said, "We'll have to leave, Willie, but we'll be back. I promise you."

CHAPTER 7

Earl Sutherton started telling his story, and soon Judge Markham forgot about supper and stopped looking at his watch. Marshal Pitts offered to light Sutherton's cigarette, but Sutherton declined, saying he didn't smoke.

"I was content to live alone," said Sutherton. "I had my little house in that pretty little valley, I had my animals, and I had peace and solitude. I was away from the rest of the human race—that race of squabbling, gossiping, selfish, cruel, small-minded, mean-spirited, ignorant, egotistical creatures." He nodded his head to the judge and the marshal and said, "Present company excepted."

The judge waved a hand in a dismissive gesture and said, "Carry on."

Sutherton carried on. "I remember once, some years back, passing through a town on a Sunday and going to church with the locals, hoping to find some help with the ugly, black sickness I carried inside. All I got out of the preacher's sermon was that there was no place in the kingdom of heaven for the likes of me. I don't know if I believe in the human soul, but I figured that if I had one, and it was beyond redemption, I could at least seek some kind of peace in this world before I passed into the next one to reap my own personal and—I admit—well-deserved whirlwind. And, peace, gentlemen, was something that, up to that time, I had seen precious little of in my life.

"I did not seek companionship, or even friendship. I only wanted solitude. I was wise enough to know that not all people are evil or hypocritical, but I had seen more than enough of both to sour me altogether on the human race. On the other hand, I knew I was no farmer, no tailor, no blacksmith, no distiller. There were things I would need that I could not produce for myself, so I would need to live near a town, and go there when I needed something. Aside from that, I intended to keep to myself. I liked to take long walks and explore the wild country outside my little kingdom. I had plenty of books to read, too. You see, gentlemen, a gunman I may be, but I am also an educated man."

"I've heard that about you," said Marshal Pitts.

"It shows in your manners and your speech," said the judge.

Sutherton gave the judge a quick smile and nod, and continued his tale. "I went to town rarely, and when I did, I was polite to everyone, but not friendly to anyone. I intended to make sure everyone knew I was not looking for friendship. One morning, I was standing in the doorway of my house and thinking about the day ahead. I had fed all the animals and milked the cow. There were a few things that needed doing, but none that needed doing right away. Except for the evening milking, and a few small chores, I would do no more work that day. I decided to take my dogs and go for a long walk in the hills. I packed some food for myself and the dogs, flipped two coins to decide which way to go, and set out.

"I began hearing the gunshots when I was no more than a mile away from my front door. They were evenly spaced—six at a time. Somebody was doing some target practice.

"'But why out here?' I wondered. I walked toward the sound, and within a short time, I was lying belly flat, peering over the crest of a hill, looking down at a little valley. There were two people down there: a young boy and an older boy. The older one was doing the shooting, while the young boy looked on."

"Now, gents, I could never explain to you just why I felt so much anger toward those two boys. I guess it was because they had interrupted the peace of my existence. I watched for a while as the older boy set up sticks of different sizes and used them as targets. He was a poor shot, and, in my opinion, he was not going to get much better unless he changed the way he was going about it.

"After a while, it looked to me like the kid felt the same way. He set the pistol down on a rock and sat down on the ground, looking unhappy. The younger lad said something, and I could clearly hear his words. He said, 'I want to go home. Are you a good shot yet?'

"The older one said, 'Let's go back to camp.'

"The younger one said, 'I don't want to go to camp. I want to go home.' And then he started to cry. The older one said, 'Willie, we don't have a home anymore.'

"Willie said, 'You said you would get to be a good shot and get our house back.'

"The older one just sat there, looking about as discouraged as anybody I've ever seen. And I've seen some people in my time who've hit bedrock, and then gone down from there. I slipped back down the hill and turned toward my house. I had lost my taste for exploring. I had only heard a part of the boys' story, but it was enough. It wasn't hard to piece the rest of it together. I had seen that story before in a hundred other places, and the thought of it made me feel mighty gloomy. It made me think about my past, and I didn't want to do that.

"I walked back to the house and went inside. I got out a book and tried to lose myself in it. About two hours later, my dogs started barking, and I went outside. Down the road—my road—I saw the two boys walking toward me. It made me angry. They had no business there. I knew they would ask me for something: food, or milk, maybe work. I had none of that that I wished to give them, and I did not want to invite them to come in and sit down for a meal, as is the custom. I just stood there and waited.

"The boys reached the house, and the dogs stopped barking and went over to them, ready to make friends. The boys rubbed their heads and spoke to them. The older boy looked up at me and said, 'Good day.'

"I just grunted and waited. I did not invite them in. He stuck out his hand and said, 'I'm Kyle Rupp. This is my brother, Willie.'

"I didn't shake the hand. I just said, 'What do you want?'

"Kyle acted a little surprised by my attitude. He said, 'I was just wonderin' if you have any .44 shells I could buy from you. I'm out.'

"'What do you want them for?' I asked him, though I already knew. He didn't seem to know what to say to this unfriendly stranger—meaning me. Finally, I guess he figured the truth could do him no harm, and he said, 'Everything we owned has been stolen from us by men who know how to use a gun. We've got nothing left.'

"'And you think you can shoot at sticks and get good enough with a gun to fight the kind of men who stole from you?'

"Well, that shocked him. I imagine he was wondering how I knew he had been shooting at sticks. He stood there, looking foolish, saying nothing. After a few moments, he said, 'Sorry to bother you,' and turned and walked away. Willie, who had been playing with the dogs, followed him, saying, 'Goodbye, doggies.' The dogs followed them for a short distance, wagging their tails.

"For the rest of the day, I tried hard to keep from thinking about those two boys. I told myself their problems were not my problems. I tried to convince myself I didn't care what happened to them, as long as they left me alone. But the image of my dogs running up to them, making friends with them, kept coming into my mind, and I remembered the words of a man I had once worked for—a man I detested. He used to say, 'People are worse than dogs, and most of them deserve to die like dogs.'

"It's funny, gents, I had never thought much about that statement, but when I thought about those boys, it struck me that I had behaved worse than my own dogs. Those boys had done nothing to deserve being treated the way I had treated them. It came to me that maybe it's not that people are worse than dogs, maybe dogs are just *better* than people."

Nate Tennet rode out of his yard, knowing he would not be returning any time soon. He had been subjected to insult and injury and the destruction of his property. He had taken all he intended to take from Lorna Fergin and her crew of hard cases. He rode, leading several horses, three of which were saddled. The other two carried bulging packs. He took his path into the hills behind his house and followed a winding trail to a fenced pasture, where he unburdened all but his own saddle horse and turned the others out into the pasture.

He carried the extra saddles and the packs into the trees, where he laid the saddles on the ground and covered them with a tarp. The packs he hung by ropes from a branch of a tall pine tree, to keep them safe from scavenging animals. Finished with these tasks, he rode away.

He found his three steady punchers, along with three other temporary hands, working in the haying. They were just coming in to their camp, which was actually a small farm that Tennet had purchased the previous year from a widower who was too old and sick to work anymore. The farm had some good hayfields, a barn in which to store the hay, and a small house for use as a line shack.

The hayers were coming in for their noon meal when Tennet rode in. He was warmly greeted with good-natured insults, as has always been the custom among working men. He got down, tied his horse, and walked to the cook fire, which was outside the house due to the warmth of the day.

He accepted a cup of coffee and began to sip. Doug Connors, the foreman of the crew, said, "We had a little trouble last night."

Tennet looked at him. "Lazy 8 kind of trouble?"

"That's what we figure. They were wearin' masks, so we didn't see any faces. They were wantin' to burn the barn. We run 'em off, but I figure they'll be back. And I expect next time, they'll bring more men."

Tennet nodded soberly. Losing the barn would be bad, but not nearly as serious as losing the precious hay that was stored inside it. Without a good stockpile of hay, he could lose a substantial portion of his herd when the heavy snows came. He told the assembled men about the wreckage at the ranch house and the burning of the barn there. "I want you to take all the hay you've stacked in the barn back out to the field and lay it in windrows. They won't be able to burn it that way."

One of the hired hands stood up and said, "Nate, I guess me and Jody will be goin' now. We've got families, and I don't like the thought of gettin' caught in the middle of a feud."

"Sure," said Tennet. "It ain't your fight. Mind finishin' out the day? They won't try anything until nightfall anyway."

The man nodded. "All right."

In the interest of getting the hay back in the field, Tennet stayed with the crew and worked with them for the rest of the day. They were able to reverse two days' worth of work that afternoon, but it left the men acting somber and displeased. They were hardworking men and took satisfaction in doing a job and doing it well. Undoing what they had accomplished, even though they were getting paid for it, was not to their liking.

It was not quite dark when the masked riders hit. Tennet had not expected them to return so soon, and he certainly had not expected them to come when it was not yet fully dark. He cursed himself for his carelessness. He and two other men were in the field, unloading a hay wagon, while the other four workers were in the barn, loading the other wagon with hay.

They came from three directions, in groups of three, shooting and shouting. Tennet had left his pistol and a carbine on the seat of the wagon, and he ran to retrieve them. The two men with him took shelter under the wagon. Tennet pulled the carbine off the wagon seat and cocked it as he put it to his shoulder. He was a dead shot with a rifle, and he knocked the lead man off his horse with his first shot, causing the two men with him to haul on the reins and pull their horses around. Tennant paid them no more attention. He swung around and snapped off a quick shot, this time hitting a rider in the arm. The man stayed in the saddle, but he and his companions, wanting no more of Nate Tennet's shooting, reined their horses around and rode away from the field.

Tennet now became aware of shooting up by the farm house, and he set off running as fast as he could toward the barn, where he knew the fight was taking place. The light of day was pretty much gone by the time he reached the fence that marked the boundary between the hayfield and the yard. He went through the gate, looking for a target. There was no more shooting, but he could hear some shouting over by the barn.

He saw movement and dim shadows, but could not identify anyone as either friend or enemy. He knew the men who had ridden away from his dangerous shooting in the hayfield would come back and congregate here very soon. He wasn't sure what to do. His men must be in the barn, but they were no longer shooting. What did that mean? Were they dead, or were they simply unable to line up on a target in the darkness?

The smell of kerosene came to his nostrils, and he knew immediately what was happening. At that moment, he saw a yellow flame start to climb up the side of the barn. A lone man, wearing a mask, was outlined against the flame, and Tennet shot him. The man staggered and fell and began crawling away from the flames, into the darkness.

There were more shouts now. Bullets were sent in Tennet's direction, but he was shrouded in darkness, and none of them hit him. He changed his position, and then saw another streak of yellow flame rising on the opposite side of the barn. Under cover of darkness, he ran toward the man he had just shot, staying out of the semicircle of light cast by the growing flames. As he drew close to the area, he dimly saw the masked rider lying on his back, gasping in pain. He was holding his pistol, but made no effort to use it when

Tennet crept up to him. Tennet took the gun out of the man's unresisting hand and stuffed it into his waistband.

The man let out a gasping shout. "He's over here." The effort seemed to have been too much for him. He moaned and fell silent.

Taking advantage of the darkness, Tennet moved away at a run, ducking behind a tree, swinging around to the back of the barn. The fire was growing, making more noise. Tennet could hear coughing coming out of the open door of the hayloft. His men must have taken refuge there from the bullets, but now the smoke and fire threatened them.

A masked man was stationed at the back of the burning structure, for the clear purpose of guarding the rear door of the barn and that of the hayloft. The men of the Lazy 8 were going to burn Tennet's men to death in the barn, or shoot them if they tried to get out. Tennet came up behind the guard, and, as he drew near, the man heard him and wheeled around. Holding the carbine by the barrel, Tennet swung it at the man's head at the same time the man saw him. It made a dull sound when it hit, and the Lazy 8 man dropped.

There was a hiss from the open door of the barn's loft, and Tennet looked up to see the face of Art Poole, one of his men, poking out of the loft door. Poole pointed downward, and Tennet saw, by the light of the growing fire, a long pole—the boom from an old hay derrick. He knew instantly what to do. It took all his strength to lift the pole and lean it against the barn wall, but when he did, it jutted up into the opening to the loft.

Immediately, men began appearing in the opening and sliding down the pole. When no more were coming down, Tennet said, "Where's Doug?"

"Dead," said Art Poole, bitterly. "Shot."

Not wanting to waste any more time, Tennet pointed and said, "Into the trees."

The men soon disappeared into the darkness. Tennet started to follow, but he realized the man he had hit with his carbine was dangerously close to the burning barn. In a few minutes, the heat would be much more intense. If the man was not dead from the blow to his head, he would soon be cooked by the heat of the fire.

Tennet ran over to him, grasped one arm, and dragged him a good distance away from the barn. The man groaned, but showed no sign of regaining consciousness. Tennet left him there and followed his hired men into the trees.

He wished he knew how the two men he had left in the hayfield had fared. He had driven the Lazy 8 men away with his accurate shooting, and he hoped they had not returned. He assumed the two men had taken advantage of the onset of darkness and slipped away from the area. It would be the logical thing to do.

Tennet now had only two hired hands left. One of his three permanent riders was dead, and all the rest of the haying crew were men and boys who had hired on just for the haying. When the group had walked in the darkness for over an hour and were relatively certain they were out of danger, Tennet took pencil and paper from his pocket and wrote a note to his friend at the bank, instructing him to pay the men's wages from his account. The temporary hired hands then went their way in the darkness, happy to be alive.

Left alone with his two remaining men, Tennet said, "You boys didn't hire on to fight a war, and I won't hold it against you if you decide to slope. I guess it's pretty clear to you by now that I have some enemies. This thing is just beginning, and there's a good chance that I and anybody that rides with me will end up like Doug."

Acting uncomfortable, Art Poole said, "Boss I hate to do it, you've been real good to work for, but—"

"It's all right, Art. Any sensible man would get as far away from here as he could." Tennet had brought some money with him, and he counted out into Art's hand the amount he was owed, and then said, "Here's some more for a horse and saddle and a few necessaries. You can hoof it over to Longhurst's and tell him I want him to sell you what you need."

"Thanks, boss. You're as square as they come."

Art wordlessly shook hands with Tennet's last remaining hired hand, Virgil Trapp, and turned and walked into the darkness.

Virgil Trapp was a lean, short, bandy-legged puncher who claimed to have been born on a horse with a rope in his hand and a chaw in his cheek. He had said nothing during Tennet's conversation with Art Poole, and he remained silent now. He had not been pleased about being sent to help with the haying two days previously, but had understood the need. Tennet's spread was new and just getting started, and sometimes the punchers had to do things they would not be required to do on a larger, more prosperous spread.

Tennet said, "You're a fool, Virge. You ought to have—"

"If I want preachin', boss, I'll go to Sunday school. And when was the last time you saw me do that?"

"You don't like preachin', how do you feel about walkin'?"

"Druther drink warm milk on a Saturday night."

"You may have noticed, Virge, that we lack horses at the present time."

"Matter of fact, I did. Do you have anything in mind?"

"I took some horses and saddles and supplies to the north pasture."

"Got to be a good six miles from here," said Virgil.

"Hence the need for walkin'."

"Do you mean to tell me they are going to do nothing?" Julia Longhurst was talking to her father about the meeting of the local cattlemen's association he had just attended.

Longhurst nodded. "The riders were wearin' masks. Sheriff Benson investigated, but he wasn't able to get very far. It's easy to say it had to be the Lazy 8, but you have to have some kind of proof."

Raising her voice, Julia said, "They've burned Nate's barn and ruined his house and killed Doug Connors. And Nate's nowhere around, which means he's either dead or on the run."

"Nobody has proof of any of that," countered Longhurst.

"That's not what's stopping them," she said acidly. "It's just that they personally haven't been affected yet. I think they're a bunch of cowards."

John Longhurst sat calmly chewing his food, and Julia went back to her cooking, but there was an angry tone in the way she stirred the food and slammed the skillet down on the cast-iron surface of the stove. Presently, she said, "How about you, Father? Are you going to help Nate, or are you going to sit around like the rest of them and watch him be destroyed?"

"Already sent two riders out to see if they can locate him and offer our help. But they'll never find him. Nate's too smart to get found."

She went to him and leaned down, wrapping her arms around his neck and kissing him on the top of the head. After a few moments, she took a seat opposite him at the table and said, "What is Lorna Fergin up to, anyway, Father? What's all this about?"

Longhurst said, "I was talkin' to Mrs. Lane this morning. She says she thinks it has to do with a railroad comin' through. She thinks Lorna knows where the tracks will be laid, and she wants that land so she can make a bundle sellin' the right-of-way to the railroad."

Julia considered this for a few moments and said, "Can't Sheriff Benson stop her?"

"How? She hasn't done anything he can prove yet. And you know he isn't going to get involved in a squabble between ranches anyway."

"This is more than a squabble."

"He doesn't see it that way."

"I think he's just afraid of the Fergins," asserted Julia.

"Of course he is. He'd be a fool not to be afraid of that murderous pack."

Julia was thoughtful for a minute, then she said, "When I heard that Saul Fergin had taken a wife, I thought maybe things would change on Lazy 8, but— "

"They have," interrupted Longhurst. "For the worse."

Deborah Pence, proprietor of the Matrimonial Correspondence Club in Chicago, Illinois, having finished her day's work, closed her desk and locked it. She then took the bundle of letters sitting on top of her desk and tied it with string, afterward leaving the small office and locking the door behind her.

At the post office, she handed the bundle to the clerk, who said, "More lonely hearts?"

Unsmiling, she said, "The world is full of them, Mr. Harris."

"And you're doing what you can to help them," said Harris, with amiable sarcasm.

Deborah Pence did not reply, nor did a smile touch her features. She started to turn away, and then, remembering something, she fished a letter out of her handbag and handed it to the clerk. Harris looked at the letter just long enough to read the name and destination. It was addressed to Lorna Fergin, in a distant western place that Harris had never heard of.

He said, "Another lonely woman just pining for a husband. Think you can find her one?"

As Deborah Pence turned away, she smiled a private smile and mumbled to herself, "I've already found her three of them."

When the envelope arrived, the return address proclaimed it to be from a Mrs. Pence at an address in Chicago, Illinois. Priscilla took it up to her bedroom and immediately opened it. It contained a letter, written in a neat, precise hand. There was no explanation. None was needed. The letter read:

I am a gentleman widower of 53 years of age, but look much younger. I am 5 feet 6 inches tall and weigh 190. I would like to correspond with a maiden or widow of good reputation and refinement who seeks a good home and a kind and lively husband. I have a good business and am well able to provide for the right woman. I prefer an attractive woman, between 25 and 40 years of age.

Priscilla was not a beautiful woman, but there was something about her face that men had always found attractive. She had learned this at an early age and had used it to her advantage ever since. Moreover, the generous proportions of her figure, as well as the ways she had of using her voice and her eyes, were enticements to which few men were immune.

She was pensive for a few minutes after reading the letter. At first, she thought the timing was not quite right; she had never before started a new courtship until after her current husband had died. But, as she thought about it, it struck her that this might be the thing she needed.

She had not been lying when she had told Jack about Saul Fergin's debts. She was certain that with Nestor Bradley's help, she could pull off this deal with the railroad, and then be a rich woman, but she needed money to operate until that happened. All the money she had gotten out of her previous husbands—both referred to her by Deborah Pence—she had used to purchase land along the route of the railroad spur. She had worried about spending it all and leaving herself no cushion, but Bradley had assured her the railroad spur was a sure thing, and he would have the final say as to the exact location of the route. Priscilla trusted no man, but in view of the fact that the money she was paid for the right-of-way was to be split with Bradley, she trusted his motives.

Besides, she reasoned, it was not good to act too hastily or seem too eager with these widowers who had money. She could take her time and act as though she were afraid of doing the wrong thing. That way, the gentleman widower would not suspect she was the kind of woman who would marry for money. Moreover, her current husband, Saul, was close to death, now. The doctor had said on his last visit that it would only be a matter of days.

Priscilla took out paper, pen, and ink, and wrote a cryptic note to Deborah Pence:

Expected event soon. Will send agreed soon after.
Most recent prospect looks good. Will accept.
P.

She then began the first draft of the first letter she would send—through Deborah Pence at the Matrimonial Correspondence Club—to the gentleman widower.

Dear Sir,
My name is Angela Williams . . .

Saul Fergin died on a Thursday and was buried the following Saturday. Priscilla put on a very convincing show of grieving, managing to call out the sympathy of all those present who didn't work for her or know her well. Of these there were only a few, the Fergins not being a popular outfit in the area, and Saul Fergin never having been at all popular with the people in the valley.

Jack Stull particularly enjoyed his sister's performance. He attended, though she had forbidden him to do so, fearing he would say or do something that would give her away. He stood apart from the rest of the group, his hat held respectfully in his hands, and tried to keep from smirking as Priscilla played her part like the professional she was.

Most of the handful of people from off the ranch who were present at Saul's funeral were there at the request of the doctor who had attended Saul during his illness. He had been taken in from the very beginning by Priscilla's act, and, being a widower, had begun to nurture his own private thoughts about the noble woman who had so diligently nursed her husband through his last days of life, and who was now so inconsolable over his death.

The doctor had convinced these few townspeople to attend the funeral, telling them that even if they hadn't cared for Saul, there must have been some good in the man if someone so noble and pure as Lorna loved him as much as she obviously did. He said that if they wouldn't attend for Saul's sake, they ought to do it for hers.

When the casket was lowered into the grave, Lorna cried out and would have fallen to the ground had not the doctor and others nearby caught her. She was assisted back to the house, where she was helped into her nightclothes by two compassionate women from town, after which the doctor gave her two doses of Ignatia Amara and told her to rest.

As he and the women walked away from the bedroom, the doctor said in a low voice, "Saul didn't deserve her."

CHAPTER 8

Life on the Lazy 8 continued just as it had during the months since Saul Fergin had become too ill to get out of bed, and his wife had begun running the affairs of the ranch. The doctor stopped by every week or so, ostensibly to check on Lorna's health. He always said he had been called out to see someone on some nearby ranch or farm who was ill, and he always stayed for tea and to chat with Lorna, who put on the appearance of grieving for the doctor's benefit.

During the first few months after Saul's death, Priscilla wrote and received several letters from the gentleman widower. All the letters went through Deborah Pence, who put those from the gentleman widower into a larger envelope, which she sealed and tied with string and addressed to Lorna Fergin.

Priscilla was occupied with the affairs of the ranch and was taking this new courtship very slowly. She knew she had to maintain a balance with the gentleman widower. If she moved too slowly, he might lose interest, but she needed to conclude the project she had begun on the Lazy 8, which involved a number of facets and was getting more complicated as time went on. Once she had possession of all the land she needed, she would be able to sell the right-of-way to the railroad, after which she would sell the ranch as well, and move on to the next piece of business, which, if all went well, would probably be the gentleman widower.

The one loose end in Priscilla's plans was Nate Tennet. Jack Stull had easily persuaded the Rupp boy to sign over his father's farm, but Tennet was proving to be a different story altogether. He had been warned in every way Priscilla could think of to stay away from the auction and leave Yellowbush Flat for the Lazy 8, but he was clearly a stubborn man. And now he had disappeared.

Priscilla had spoken to Jack and to Dale Ramsey, making it clear to both of them that she wanted Nate Tennet out of the way, and she didn't care how it was done. Ramsey had merely nodded in the sullen way he had, which only increased her distrust of him each time he did it. Jack had smiled wickedly and said, "Whatever you say, Sis. All we got to do is find him. I'll take care of the rest."

"Well, that's the problem, isn't it?" she said sarcastically. "I could take care of him myself, if I knew where he was. I really don't know what you or Ramsey are good for. You both just sit around doing nothing about Tennet, like you expect him to ride in and say, 'Here I am, did someone want to shoot me?'"

Jack scowled at her for a moment and walked out. Priscilla watched him go, hating him worse than ever, wishing he had not found her. She reflected on this situation for several minutes, realizing that he would always find her. He had a way of always turning up when she was about to make some money, wanting to share in it. He did no work on the ranch, and he came and went as he pleased. He made no effort to become acquainted with any of the hands, or even to be polite to them. No one had told anyone on the ranch that he was her brother, but the fact was generally understood, in part because of Jack's privileged status, and in part because of a marked family resemblance. Dale Ramsey resented Jack and made no secret of it, but he had never openly challenged the man, and this was, again, because of the man's relationship to the boss.

Priscilla was well aware that, like her brother, she had no friends on the ranch. The men resented her because she was a woman, and she was a newcomer. They had all hired on to work for Saul Fergin, and now they were working for his widow. A few of them had left after Saul's funeral, but the rest had stayed, knowing they would not be able to get jobs anywhere nearby.

The Lazy 8 and its riders did not enjoy a good reputation in the area. Any time one of the other ranches found it was missing cattle, the Lazy 8 was the first suspect, and, as Jack had informed Priscilla, the suspicions were generally not without foundation. Priscilla knew she was the boss of a pack of ruffians and hard cases, and the fact did not displease her. They were just the kind of men she needed at present. The only problem was they were not loyal to her.

Nate Tennet was no coward, but neither was he a fool. He had been known to be impulsive at times, but this was war, and he was wise enough to know that impulsiveness had no place in such a conflict.

There was no point in winning a battle if it cost you the war. He knew the Lazy 8 would be hunting him and Virgil, and he decided the best course would be to hide out until they gave up the search. He would fight the Lazy 8 to his last breath. They had killed one of his hands, and tried to burn the others to death. They had beaten him and wrecked his cabin. Oh, yes. He would fight them, but he would wait until after the auction. He was determined to own Yellowbush Flat.

Earl Sutherton discontinued his narrative long enough to ask if the handcuff could be shifted to the other hand for a while.

"If he came in here on his own accord," said the judge, "I don't see why he needs to be chained up like that."

Marshal Pitts thought about this for a minute and said, as a warning to the prisoner, "All right then. I'll just keep my gun handy." He unlocked the handcuff and set it on his desk.

Nodding to the judge, Sutherton said, "Thanks." He continued. "The next day, I went to the spot where the two boys were camped and rode right into their camp. They looked surprised, and a bit worried, too. They were two unhappy-looking boys, for sure. I handed Kyle—the older boy—a box of .44 shells and said, 'You can have these, but they won't do you a bit of good. You're going about it all wrong.'

"The kid didn't seem to know what to say. He stood there looking at me for maybe half a minute, and I could see he was at the end of his rope. If it hadn't been for that kid brother of his, he could have left the valley and started on a life for himself, but as it was, he was damned if he stayed, damned if he left—he was damned any way he turned. I saw all this in his eyes, and I couldn't help feeling a little sorry for him."

Sutherton smiled and shook his head, "I didn't like it a bit, but there was no denying I was turning soft. I told myself I needed to ride away, but I heard myself telling the kid I would teach him how to use a gun. Well, you would've thought I had just told him I was giving him a gold mine. He was so appreciative, I thought he was going to cry. We started that very day with his lessons."

Sutherton stood up to stretch his legs and adjust his pants, causing Marshal Pitts to put his hand on his gun.

"No need to be nervous, Marshal. I didn't turn myself in so I could try to get away on foot, unarmed, with you shooting at me."

Pitts relaxed a little, and Sutherton sat down again and resumed his tale. "Well, gents, I worked with that boy for two weeks, and I'll have to admit he improved a little, but it was pretty clear from the start he'd never be much of a hand with a gun. I tried to tell him that several times, but he was determined to do it, and he just kept saying, 'I'll get it. It will just take practice. Be patient with me.' After a few days, he ran me out of bullets, and I had to go to town to buy more. He had a little money from the small amount his enemies had given him for his farm, and he made me take some of it for the bullets. He was not quick to accept charity. I tried every trick I knew to teach that boy how to shoot straight and fast, and he did get better, but it wasn't enough. Problem was, I couldn't get him to believe he would never be good enough. He said, 'Sir, I'm going to do it with or without you. I'll get good with a gun, and I'll get my farm back.' There wasn't much I could do except keep teaching him as best I could."

Sutherton looked at the marshal and said, "I'm a little dry from all this talking. You wouldn't have a sip of whiskey, would you?"

The marshal and the judge looked at each other, and the judge shrugged. "I wouldn't mind a nip."

The marshal produced a bottle with a small amount of whiskey in the bottom. He found three glasses and divided the whiskey equally among them. Sutherton accepted his glass, tasted the whiskey, made a face, and said, "I'd be willing to pay for a full bottle, if you gents wouldn't mind. That way, we could all wet our tonsils more thoroughly."

The judge, too, had tasted his small measure of Marshal Pitts' liquor, and he said, "I think that would be all right."

Sutherton stood up and started to reach into his pocket.

"Wait!" ordered the marshal. He walked over and patted the pocket, then nodded to Sutherton.

Sutherton produced the money and said, "Get the best they've got, Marshal."

Pitts gave his pistol to the judge and said, "I'll be right back."

Sutherton sat there, a half smile on his face. "The marshal doesn't trust me."

The judge chuckled. "No, he doesn't."

"Doesn't matter; I'm not here for him, anyway."

If the judge thought this was an odd statement, he made no comment to that effect.

Marshal Pitts returned and poured the whiskey. "Never thought I'd become an errand boy for a killer."

Sutherton took a generous sip of the whiskey and said, "That's better. My father always said, 'If you can't afford good whiskey, don't drink whiskey at all.'"

There was a brief silence as the men savored their drinks, and, finally, Sutherton started talking again. "After a couple of weeks, I told the kid I needed a rest. He said he would keep practicing, and asked me if I would come back after my rest and tell him if he had improved any. I agreed to that. I was running out of supplies, and I decided to go to town. I also knew, though the boys hadn't said anything, that they were getting low on food, so I figured I'd pick up a few things for them, too. Anyhow, on the trail to town, I saw a rider coming toward me. That was nothing unusual—it was a pretty well traveled trail—but there was something familiar about the man. When he got closer, I recognized him. It was Jack Stull. Heard of him?"

The marshal nodded. The judge said, "Not sure. Sounds kind of familiar."

"Gunman," said Pitts to the judge. "A killer. One of the worst."

Sutherton nodded. "One of the worst, indeed. I never had any use for men like him."

He took a sip of the whiskey, savored it for a moment, and continued. "He recognized me too, and we sat there on our horses for a moment, each of us waiting to see what the other would do. Finally, Stull said, 'How've you been, Earl?'

"I told him I'd been fine. He said, 'You doin' a job hereabouts?' I said no. I wasn't about to tell him any more than I had to. We talked a bit about people we had known—most of them dead—and we parted company, each of us with his hand on his gun and looking over his shoulder until we had put some distance between us. I was a couple of miles down the trail before I realized that it must have been Stull who had gone to the Rupp farm and forced Kyle to sign the deed over to him. And I knew that if that crazy kid was planning on going up against Jack Stull, he was as good as dead already."

Sutherton could see that his audience was hooked. Both the marshal and the judge were listening with rapt attention to his tale, and he was enjoying telling it as much as they were enjoying hearing it. He said, "That night I rode over and told Kyle I would meet him the next morning at our usual place, but earlier than usual. I told him to be there just before dawn.

"Next morning, I was there before the boys arrived. I stepped out from behind a rock, wearing gray clothes and two pistols, and without saying a word, I started shooting at Kyle."

"You were shooting at him?" said the judge, disapprovingly.

The marshal understood, and put a calming hand on the judge's arm.

Sutherton said, "Not exactly at him, but near him. I was putting bullets right past his ears, shooting as fast as I could thumb back the hammers and pull the triggers. You should have seen that boy. He clapped his hand on his pistol and got the front sight hung up in the holster. He was jerking and tugging on it, swearing all the while. He got his gun out and then dropped it on the ground. He picked it up and cocked it and fired a shot into the dirt in front of him. All the while, I was putting shots so close to him, he could feel them flying past. When he finally got his gun pointed toward me, his hand was shaking so bad that he wouldn't have hit me if I'd been three feet away. That was when I stopped firing. I was out of bullets anyway.

"I said, 'Don't shoot, kid. It's just me.' He was still swearing, and he swore some more, right at me, but I could tell he was relieved to learn I was not an enemy. He tried to holster his pistol, but his hand was shaking so bad he almost dropped it again. I said, 'Kid, you're not a gunslinger, and you never will be. We've been working on this for weeks now, and you're getting pretty good at hitting cans and sticks and firewood, but being a good shot is not the most important part of being a gunfighter. You just learned what is. Do you understand what I'm telling you?'

"He nodded and went over and sat down on a rock, hanging his head down like a whipped dog. I didn't feel guilty about what I had done to him, because I knew I had saved his life. I said, 'Son, you need to leave the gun fighting to gunfighters.' I left him there, sitting on that rock, looking about as sorrowful as a man can get and not die. You would have felt sorry for him, gents."

"Did you feel sorry for him?" asked the judge.

"Me? Why, Your Honor, I'm a hardened killer."

CHAPTER 9

Priscilla ordered Dale Ramsey to station men along every trail and road into town early in the morning on the day of the land auction. The men were to be told to watch for Nate Tennet and stop him by any means necessary, even if it meant shooting him.

Priscilla was not happy about missing the auction, but she had received an urgent telegram from Nestor Bradley, requiring her to meet him in Topeka to discuss their plans. She left the following day—two days before the auction. Before departing, she told Ramsey how much he was authorized to bid for Yellowbush Flat, and made the necessary arrangements with the bank.

"That's three times as much as that piece of land is worth," the banker told her.

This was not news to Priscilla, and she was confident that no one bidding against Ramsey would go as high as that amount, but she was taking no chances. It was imperative that she own Yellowbush Flat.

Dale Ramsey was taking no chances either, and he stationed his men at dusk the night before, and then went into town and booked himself a room in the hotel. He planned to spend the evening and most of the night cruising around town, watching out for Nate Tennet. Lorna had not told him why she so desperately wanted to own Yellowbush Flat, but she had made it very clear that it was of the utmost importance, and Ramsey had the feeling that if he allowed Tennet to slip past him, even if the rancher didn't outbid him, it would cost him his job as foreman of the Lazy 8.

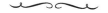

Nate Tennet expected Lorna Fergin to take precautions to keep him from bidding on Yellowbush Flat, so he rode to town early on the day before the auction and took a room at the hotel, leaving his horse with a friend in town. He watched now from his hotel room as

Ramsey, with three other men, rode into town, surreptitiously scanning the faces on the boardwalks and streets. He smiled, knowing they were looking for him, and when Ramsey and his men took the room next to his, it amused Tennet even more.

As a precaution, Tennet had used a fictitious name when signing the hotel register, and he was glad now that he had. Ramsey would never have overlooked that detail. Tennet had also made arrangements to have his meals brought up to him. He had no intention of showing his face before the auction started tomorrow morning.

He lay on his back on the bed, thinking of all that had transpired in recent weeks. He and Virgil Trapp had been camping in a secluded spot known only to them, waiting for the day of the auction to arrive. Virgil had wanted to retaliate against the Lazy 8. He advocated burning every barn, line shack, and haystack the Lazy 8 owned. But Tennet knew that Dale Ramsey would be expecting retaliation and would be waiting. "Anyway," he argued, "We wouldn't gain anything by it."

"I would," countered Virgil.

"What?"

"It'd make me feel real good."

Tennet shook his head. "No. We've got to fight smart. We won't do what they expect us to do. We'll wait and see what they do next."

As he thought about it now, Tennet knew that by being here in town, and by bidding on Yellowbush Flat tomorrow, he was being predictable. But there was no way to avoid that except by not bidding on the property, and that would be unacceptable to him. He had briefly considered arranging for someone else to bid in his place, but had rejected the idea. Lorna Fergin's men had attacked him, they had burnt his barn and wrecked his house, and they had killed one of his men. He wanted to beat her out of the piece of land she so coveted, and he wanted her to know it was he who had done it.

He lay back on the bed, his hands behind his head. He was tired of thinking of his enemies and their plans, so he purposely turned his mind to more pleasant thoughts. He thought about Julia Longhurst. He wondered what she was doing right now. She had been frequently in his thoughts since the day he had awoken to see her by the fire she had made, sitting on his saddle. She had done an act of kindness that day. She had been concerned about him and about his horse, and had done what she could for them.

She was like that, he knew. She was known in the valley for her kind acts. In that way, she was like her father. She was like him in another way, too, Tennet could tell: She was a fighter.

Oh, well, he told himself, as he had a hundred times before, Julia Longhurst disliked him and probably always would. He needed to forget her. He tried to push the image of her face out of his mind, and after a while, he fell asleep.

Jack Stull watched as Ramsey and several other riders rode away. Stull was not happy about recent events on the Lazy 8. Priscilla had gone to meet with Nestor Bradley, and had pointedly gone alone. Ramsey had ridden out, taking with him a group of men that did not include Jack Stull. They were treating him as if he had no importance at all here on this ranch, and the resentment that had been festering in Stull's mind grew a little larger.

It was dusk. Julia Longhurst and her father were sitting in the restaurant across the street from the hotel, waiting to order their supper, when Julia looked out the window and saw a man looking out of an upper window of the hotel. She recognized him instantly. It was Nate Tennet.

She had been worried about Tennet, and had thought about him often since the day she had found him sleeping beneath the pine tree, his face bruised and swollen. Julia had had feelings for him since she was a young girl. She had known in those days that she was too young for him, but now that she was older, the four-year gap between their ages didn't seem so significant.

The off-hand comment he had made—about her looking like a shovel handle in a dress—that she had reminded him of on their last meeting, would not have hurt her so badly had it not been for the feelings she had for him, and she had carried her childish grudge for years.

She knew, as did everyone in the valley, about the escalating feud between Tennet and the Lazy 8, and she knew about the fight at

Pruitt's hay barn. After that fight, Tennet had disappeared. Julia was relieved now to know he was alive and safe, and she wanted to talk to him. She had the need to tell him that the quarrel they had had when they last met was due to childishness on her part, and was insignificant compared to recent events. Most of all, she had the need to tell him she was his friend, and if it came to taking sides, she would always be on his. She decided to talk to him this very night.

Julia had grown up around men. She had been raised by her father, and though there had been many women in her life—family friends, friends from school, women at church—all of whom had taken an interest in the girl and tried to do what they could to help and educate her, the fact remained that she had grown up around men. She understood the finer points of propriety and etiquette, but they were not all ingrained habits, and so it was in keeping with her fundamental nature that, after their meal, when her father left to go to his favorite saloon, telling her to walk down the street to the home of her friend, Anne Davis, and spend the evening there, she should walk over to the hotel and ask the desk clerk if he would send someone up to tell Nate Tennet she was waiting in the lobby and would like to talk to him.

The desk clerk's brow furrowed, and he said, "I don't recall a Nate Tennet taking a room today." He looked at the register and said, "No. There's definitely no Tennet registered."

It struck Julia at that moment that Nate was probably being cautious and had registered under a false name to keep his enemies from knowing he was in town. She said, "Sorry. I must have been mistaken."

As she turned to leave, she noticed a man standing nearby, carrying a handful of cigars he had obviously just purchased. He had been looking at her, but quickly looked away when she turned to look at him. He walked away and ascended the stairs. Julia had seen the man before. He worked for the Lazy 8.

A surge of fear washed through her. She had unwittingly revealed Tennet's presence to his enemies. She turned back to the desk clerk and said, "This is very important. The room on the upper floor with the window directly above us—which room is that?"

The clerk hesitated for just a moment and said, "Room Three."

"And the man who just went up? The one carrying the cigars—which room is he in?"

"Room Five. Right next door."

Julia's heart seemed to stop for a few moments. The whole world seemed to stop. "What have I done?" she murmured, as she turned and left the lobby.

It seemed darker outside than it had when she had gone into the hotel. She stood by the corner of the building and tried to think of what to do, her mind and heart racing as if trying to outdo each other. After a moment, she turned and hurried back into the hotel. The clerk was sitting behind the desk, writing. He looked up when she entered.

She said, "Are there any rooms available on the second floor?"

"Certainly. Number four—

She interrupted him, "I mean next to Room Three."

The clerk made no effort to disguise his disapproval, but he let her sign the register and gave her the key to Room One. "Top of the stairs," he said.

Thanking him, Julia took the key and made an effort to keep from appearing anxious. She wanted to run up the stairs and knock on Tennet's door, but she knew that such behavior might bring his enemies out of their room. Forcing herself to walk slowly, she climbed the stairs and opened the door to Room One. It had been a hot day, and the air in the closed-up room was stifling. She walked straight across the room to the window, raised it, and pulled the curtains aside to allow the cool evening air into the room.

She leaned out over the narrow porch roof just below the window, and turned her head to look at the window of the room next to hers. That window was open too. It would be open, of course, on a cool night like this after a hot day. All the windows in town would open to invite the delicious cool air into the houses and businesses.

A faint light came out of Tennet's window, and Julia knew he had a lamp burning. She pulled her head back in and went to the bed. She lay down on it and felt the uncomfortable warmth that it had retained and probably would not give up for hours. Nevertheless, she lay back in the darkness and waited. She would wait until she felt safe in doing so, and then she would warn Tennet.

After about an hour, Julia felt the time had come. She went to the window and started to climb out onto the porch roof. As she did so, she turned to look to the side and was shocked to see a man holding a pistol, standing outside Tennet's now-dark window. He was carefully lifting a booted foot over the sill when he heard Julia's shocked intake of breath.

On the spur of the moment, Julia could think of only one thing to do to warn Tennet. She started to scream. The man also had a snap decision to make, and he rushed over to her and tried to push her back into her room. He had holstered his gun, and was attempting to put his hand over her mouth to stop her screaming. She resisted, pulling away from him and trying to put the heavy curtains between them—the only defense she could think of.

The man tried to pull the curtains out of her grip, and for a brief moment, the two of them engaged in a tug-of-war with the curtains, until the curtain rod broke, and the man fell backward and slid off the roof. Julia fell backward, as well, into the room. She put out a hand to break her fall, and felt something snap. The pain was instantaneous. She cried out and cradled her arm, holding her hand around the painful spot. She immediately pulled herself to her feet and carefully put her head out the window.

A man's head and shoulders extended out the window of Room Five. She pulled her head in quickly, reasonably confident the man had not seen her. Her arm throbbed fiercely, and she groaned softly from the pain. She was trying to decide what to do, when she heard a faint sound next to her, and it startled her. She spun around, and a strong, rough hand covered her mouth. But her fear was instantly dispelled when she heard a soft voice say, "It's me, Nate Tennet."

The hand was removed from her mouth, and she exhaled. Her heart was pounding. She went to the door and checked it.

Tennet whispered, "I locked it." He lowered the window and locked it, too, saying nothing about the lack of curtains on the window. He said, "I hope you don't mind, but I need to stay here until morning. Is there someplace else you can go?"

Julia didn't trust her voice, and she did not know if it was because of the pain in her arm, or fright, or something else. "How did you know this was my room?" she asked.

"I looked out my window when I heard the screaming, and caught a glimpse of you when you were wrestling with the big fellow. I guess he mistook your window for mine. I was going to come help you, but then he fell backward and went over the edge."

There were the sounds of footsteps on the stairs, and then in the hallway outside. Julia barely noticed. Her pain was all she could think of. She finally said to Tennet, "I shouldn't be here with you."

"I know. I'm sorry to do this."

"I . . ." She could think of nothing to say. The pain in her arm was threatening to overwhelm her.

There were voices in the hallway; someone was outside her door. "Everything all right, miss?"

Tennet was beside her. "Say yes," he whispered.

"Yes," she called out, realizing that her voice sounded odd. She added, "There was a man outside my window, but he's gone."

The footsteps went away. Tennet went to the window and spent a few minutes rigging the curtain rod so it would hold the curtains up to cover the window. Afterward, he lit the lamp on top of the bureau. When the yellow light flooded the room, he turned to look at Julia and immediately said, "You're pale."

She sat in the chair opposite the bed and said, "I have to go." She tried to hold her arm in a normal posture so he would not know she was injured, and it made the pain worse.

Tennet said, "Yes, of course. I'll turn out the lamp."

When the room was dark again, he said, "Do you have somewhere you can go this late?"

She nodded. "Anne Davis."

"Sorry to put you out. I'll leave early in the morning. Thanks again."

Once again, she could think of nothing to say, so she simply went to the door, slipped out into the dark hallway, and descended the stairs. She walked to the doctor's house. There was light inside. With her good hand, she rapped lightly on the door. The doctor's wife answered and exclaimed, "Julia, you look awful. What's wrong?"

Julia held up her hand, "It's my arm. I fell."

"Come in, dear. You must lie down. I'll make you some tea. Wilbur will be with you shortly. He's attending a man with a broken leg and a bad cut on his head. He fell off the roof of the hotel. Can you imagine that?"

After Julia left, Tennet sat in the darkness, immersed in his thoughts. He had never deluded himself that Julia liked him, but her behavior tonight had convinced him that she truly loathed him. She had acted distant and . . . he tried to think of the right word to characterize her attitude tonight, and could only come up with the fact that she seemed to find his presence distasteful. He asked himself if that could have been due to the fact that the two of them being alone in the room together was inappropriate, and rejected the thought. The Julia he knew would have simply said it was inappropriate and told him to leave, or left herself. She would not have acted so strangely about it.

He felt that it shouldn't bother him that Julia disliked him so much, and it was upsetting to him that it did. He tried to analyze the reasons behind his feelings, tried to determine if it was just his masculine vanity that was upset by her attitude, and concluded, to his dismay, that it was much more than that. Yes, he admitted with dismal candor, it was much more than that.

He realized that he had preferred Julia's former anger with him to her attitude tonight. Anger could be overcome, and even people who cared about each other could become angry with one another. But tonight, Julia had made him feel despised and unimportant.

Insignificant was the word. He finally had it. She had acted as though he were insignificant to her.

The next morning dawned gray and dreary, and Tennet, having sat up all night with a gun in his hand, found himself wishing he could sleep instead of going to a land auction. Nevertheless, he washed up and shaved and put on clean clothes.

Dale Ramsey, accompanied by one of his riders, arrived at the courthouse ahead of Tennet, and he kept his gloomy countenance turned away, though Tennet knew the man was well aware of his presence.

The bidding started low, and Ramsey quickly took it up high in an obvious attempt to exceed Tennet's maximum budget and end the bidding quickly. But, when Tennet stayed with him, always bidding a little more than Ramsey's last bid, Ramsey started to sweat.

John Longhurst was in the crowd, and he watched Ramsey with hidden amusement as the bids went higher and higher. Longhurst perceived that the Lazy 8 foreman was approaching his limit. He wondered what Lorna Fergin would say to the unfortunate man when she learned he had lost the bidding.

At last, the gavel came down, and Tennet was the new owner of Yellowbush Flat. Ramsey shot him a dark look, filled with the promise of vengeance, and Tennet smiled at him, simulating that magnanimity that comes so easily to winners of contests. A close observer would have noticed that Nate Tennet and John Longhurst completely avoided looking at each other—as co-conspirators often do.

CHAPTER 10

The calamity that John Longhurst had predicted would befall Dale Ramsey when Lorna Fergin learned of his failure at the auction was in no way worse than the actual event. Lorna screamed and raged and told Ramsey he was fired. She called him every vulgar name she could think of, then told him to get off her ranch immediately or she would have him shot—no, she would shoot him herself.

Not wanting to miss the fireworks, Jack Stull had installed himself in a chair in a corner before Ramsey arrived, and he thoroughly enjoyed the show. When Ramsey turned to leave, red-faced and breathing hard from suppressed anger, Stull said, "Mommy whipped her little boy."

Ramsey had reached his limit. Hurling curses at Stull, he wheeled and started toward the man. Stull stood up and put his hand on his gun butt. Ramsey was not wearing a gun, but his anger overcame common sense, and he did not stop until Lorna barked, "Stop it, you two. Jack, sit down. I want no gunplay here."

Stull did not sit. He brushed past Ramsey and stomped across the room and out the door. Lorna handed Ramsey an envelope and said, "Here's your pay, though you don't deserve it. You ought to pay me, instead."

Ramsey took the envelope, tramped to the bunkhouse, stuffed his things into his war bag, and went to the corral, where the hostler, on orders from Lorna, had his horse saddled and waiting. He left the yard on the run, and did not slow down until he hit the first fork in the road, which was situated in a wooded area down in a shallow swale. He sat there, not knowing where to go now. He was out of a job and not well liked in the area. He doubted any outfit around here would hire him.

There was a voice behind him, and he reined his horse around in alarm. It was Stull, coming out of the trees on his horse. Stull approached, his intentions obvious, and said, "I've never let any man talk to me the way you did and live."

Ramsey was not afraid of Stull. He had plenty of confidence in his own skill with a gun, and, in his angry state, he welcomed the impending fight. He said, "You decide how you want to handle this. I'll fight you with my fists or with my gun. Makes no difference to me how I kill you."

Stull gave a wicked smile, and went for his gun.

Ramsey's hand dropped to his own gun, and it was just clearing the holster when Stull's bullet hit him and knocked him off his horse. He fell on his back and lay unmoving. Stull walked his horse over and sat there, looking down at him, a particular kind of smile on his face. He got off his horse and went to Ramsey, found the envelope with his pay, and took it. He then rummaged through Ramsey's war bag and found some money Ramsey had saved up. He pocketed this, too.

Finished, he got on his horse and rode toward town, leaving Ramsey's horse standing in the road, still saddled.

"Well, gents," said Earl Sutherton to Judge Markham and Marshal Pitts. "It was about that time that I decided it was time to put my ear to the ground. I'd been around enough to smell trouble when it was afoot, and I could smell it now, mighty strong. I started going to town nearly every day. I made a few friends, mostly people who worked in stores and the like—folks that knew all the gossip and the latest news.

"The biggest news was that Nate Tennet had bought Yellowbush Flat—and paid a high price—and from what I had learned about him, he didn't have that kind of money. Everybody was asking where it came from. They all figured somebody was backing him.

"The other big news was that Lorna Fergin had fired Dale Ramsey, and no one knew where he had gone. No one really cared where he had gone—except for me. I knew where he was, and I cared only because it was forced on me."

"Forced on you?" asked the judge. "How was that?"

Sutherton took another sip of whiskey, looked appreciatively at the glass, and said, "One night there was a knock on my door. Truth be told, it sounded more like a kick than a knock, and that's because a kick is exactly what it was.

"I slipped out my back door with my gun in my hand, and quietly moved around the side of the house, where I looked around the corner to see what was going on. It was Ramsey—though I didn't know him at the time—sitting on his horse, slumped over. He was right next to my door, and about every thirty seconds, he mustered the strength to kick it. He was that weak.

"I went to him and helped him down out of the saddle, and even in the dark, I could tell he was shot. Well, gents, we've already established that I'm not one of those kind-hearted souls that goes around helping people who are in trouble. I'm a retired gunman, not a do-gooder."

Sutherton looked at his audience of two, and saw no dissenting headshakes. He said, "My first thought was to let the man die, and then keep his horse and saddle."

He paused again—for effect—then continued, "But on some silly impulse, I took him inside and made a bed for him on the floor. I hadn't gone so soft as to give him my own bed. I took a look at his wound. It was bad, but I'd seen worse on men who had pulled through. I figured he had an even chance of living or dying, and I told myself I didn't much care which it was. But then, I got to thinking about it, and I realized the ground around my place is pretty rocky, and I dislike digging under the best of circumstances. If Ramsey died, I'd have to dig a grave in that rocky soil, so I decided to take care of him as best I could and save myself some sweat. After all, if I'd wanted to dig in the dirt, I would've become a farmer, not a gunman.

"As it turned out, being a nurse isn't the easiest thing in the world, either, but I figure anything's got to be easier than farming."

He laughed, "Guess I got a little off the subject, there, didn't I? Well, Ramsey later told me that after getting fired from the Lazy 8, he got in a gunfight with Jack Stull. Foolish thing to do. I could have told him Stull would be a real hard man to outdraw. Anyway, Stull had thought he was dead and just left him lying there. When Stull was gone, Ramsey managed to get back on his horse. He rode to the nearest house—my house—and kicked on the door."

Sutherton paused and put down his empty whiskey glass. He looked at his two listeners and said, "Is anybody hungry?"

"I am," said the judge.

The marshal chuckled in resignation and stood up. "I'll go down to the Jumpin' Frog and get Andy to make us up some sandwiches and milk."

After the land auction, Tennet went back home, figuring the Lazy 8 would have no reason to hunt him now. He and Virgil began riding around the spread, checking on the cattle, the graze, the haystacks, and the watering holes.

Four days later, Lorna Fergin rode in to Tennet's yard, smiling as if they were old friends. Tennet came out and stood silently, his arms crossed. Virgil had spotted Lorna when she was far off, and was watching from a window.

Still smiling, Lorna said, "There's no need to greet me with that scowl. We're neighbors."

"What can I do for you?" said Tennet, coldly.

"The first thing would be to invite me to get down. Isn't that the proper way to treat a guest?"

Tennet's sense of hospitality, like that of all westerners, was strong, and it rebelled against the way he was treating Lorna. He deliberated in his mind for a few moments, finally saying, "Go ahead. Get down."

They walked into the house, and Tennet waved her to the table. "Coffee?"

"Yes, please. Black."

He took the pot off the stove and poured two cups, handing her one. He stood opposite her, waiting.

She said, "You could sit. I'm not dangerous."

He sat.

She said, "Mostly, I came to apologize."

"Apologize?"

"I've been a terrible neighbor. I . . ." She hesitated. "Mr. Tennet . . . may I call you Nate?"

"Suit yourself."

She continued. "I was raised a certain way, and I am coming to realize it was wrong. My parents were angry and bitter people, and I've been behaving the way they always did. It was all I knew. Lately, I've been reading the Bible, and I've decided to try to be a different person. I'm going to start going to church and . . . oh, I know it sounds . . . well, hypocritical, but . . ." She smiled. "I won't ask you for an answer right now, please don't say anything, but I would like you to think about forgiving me, Nate."

Tennet said, "I'll think on it."

She smiled and nodded. "That's good enough for now." She said, "I don't know if you know it, but I've fired that horrible Dale Ramsey. He did so many awful things without my knowledge. I understand he wrecked this place and burned your barn. I intend to make that up to you, if you will let me."

"Whatever suits you."

She gave a faint smile of resignation and said, "I understand. These things take time." She stood up.

Tennet stood too.

She walked over to him and extended her hand. He took it, and she held his hand between her two, looking into his eyes. "Nate, I think you and I could become very good friends."

She turned and walked out to her horse. He helped her up, and she smiled down at him and said, "Thank you for not shooting me when I rode up. You would have had every right to do so." She reined the horse around and rode out of the yard.

When she was gone, Virgil came out of the house and stood beside Tennet, watching the fading dust kicked up by Lorna Fergin's horse. Neither man said anything for a while. Finally, Tennet said, "Well, let's get to work."

Priscilla waited by the tree next to the road four nights in a row, remaining there for several hours each time. Finally, on the fourth night, her persistence was rewarded.

Tennet had decided to go to town this night. He was feeling lonely and in need of some companionship other than that of the laconic Virgil Trapp. As he approached the big tree about two miles down the trail from his house, he heard sobbing. He rode closer, and in the moonlight, he saw a horse.

The sobbing continued. It was a woman's voice, and her form could be seen as he drew near. She was facing the tree, leaning against it. Tennet reined in, and said, "Beg pardon, ma'am. Is there anything I can do?"

She turned to face him.

He dismounted, and repeated, "Anything I can do?"

She cried out, "Oh," and ran to him, wrapping her arms around him and burying her face in his chest, sobbing. Tennet realized it was Lorna Fergin. They remained like this for some time, until her crying finally ceased.

She said, "Oh, Nate. I'm so glad it's you. It's as if heaven sent you." She pulled back, remaining just a few inches away from him, and wiped her eyes with a handkerchief. "I'm sorry." She leaned forward again, embracing him and resting her head once again on his chest. "I'm so alone, Nate. I have had to try to be strong, but I'm so tired of being alone. You're a man. You wouldn't understand how it is to be afraid."

"Sure I would."

She looked up, her face close to his. "You're so kind, and I've been so . . . so hard. I'll never forgive myself for what the Lazy 8 has done to you."

"Don't worry about it."

"I don't know how to describe how I feel right now," she said. "I feel safe. For the first time in a very long time, I feel safe. Oh, Nate, thank you for your kindness." Her voice had grown lower, softer, alluring.

She reached up and put her hands on his cheeks, caressing them. She pulled his face down to hers and kissed his lips long and gently. When she pulled away, she said, "I'm sorry. You probably think I'm forward."

He pulled her to him and held her tightly. He said, "I love you, Lorna."

"You do? After all that has happened, you love me?"

"Yes."

She gave a cry that sounded like joy and pulled his face down again, pressing her body against him. She kissed him again, moving her head and making little moans.

When the kiss was over, she said, "I love you too, my dear. I hadn't dared to hope . . ."

"Will you marry me?" he said.

She pulled away, looking up at him. "It's so sudden, my love. Is it proper?"

"I don't care. Let's get married."

She hesitated for a moment, and suddenly, she laughed. "Yes, my love. Yes, yes. Let's get married."

He said, "We'll go to San Francisco. We'll stay in the finest hotels, eat the finest food, drink hundred-year-old wine. We'll sail to the orient and then to Europe. We'll stay away for a year."

"But, Nate, can you afford all that?"

"I can now."

"What do you mean, now?"

"I sold Yellowbush Flat to a fellow from the railroad."

In an instant, her demeanor changed from sunshine to ice. She backed away from him, cursing more foully than any man he had ever known. Her hand went to the pocket of her dress and came out holding a small pistol.

As she brought the gun up, he stepped forward and caught her hand, pushing it upward. When she fired, the gun was high enough so the bullet only grazed the top of his shoulder. He held her hand tightly, and when her other hand came out of her pocket holding a knife, he was ready. He grasped the hands and squeezed until she cried out and dropped the weapons.

She screamed vulgarities at him and tried to kick him. He held her hands until she stopped trying to get away, and then pulled her with him as he moved toward his horse. There, he released her, stepped into the saddle, and spurred away.

"You'll never be able to use that land," she screeched at him. "I'll never let you set a foot on my range. You just wasted a lot of money."

"Goodbye, my love," he called back to her. "I'll miss your sweet kisses."

As Tennet rode away, he felt mildly ashamed. He had no remorse about what he had done. Lorna Fergin was a poisonous woman, and she deserved what she had gotten, and more. It was what he had felt that he was ashamed of. Lorna was not a beautiful woman, not like Julia Longhurst, but there was something about her face and her figure that had stirred him. He had enjoyed the kisses, enjoyed feeling her press against him, even though he had known all along what game she was playing. He had wished it could be real, had fantasized just a little that Lorna was not lying.

"A man hadn't ought to get as lonely as I am," he said aloud to himself. "It ain't healthy." He rode all the way to town with these thoughts in his mind, and once there, he thought about turning around and riding back to his place. He realized it wasn't just company he was seeking; he wanted to see Julia.

It would be a long ride out to the Longhursts', and it would be a futile one. Julia had made it clear that she had no interest in him; indeed, she had little regard for him at all. He went to the doctor's house and got his shoulder wound bandaged. The doctor asked how he had acquired the wound, and Tennet said, "It was a snake."

From the doctor's house, he went to his favorite Saloon, played a few hands of poker with some men he knew there, lost some money, and rode back home.

In all, it had been a singularly unsatisfying night.

Julia Longhurst and Anne Davis were sitting on the front porch of the Davis home, enjoying the cool night air. Julia had been staying with Anne and her family while her broken arm healed. This evening, the two friends had been reading poetry by the light of a single candle, and they had talked, as friends will, about a multitude of subjects.

A rider started to pass in front of the house, and another rider, going the opposite direction, spoke to him. "Howdy, Nate." The two men stopped to talk for a few minutes, and their voices came clearly to the ears of the young women. Presently, the men parted, and Julia and Anne watched as Tennet rode past, not looking toward them. After he had passed, Julia looked at Anne to find the girl intently watching her face. Julia blushed and looked away.

"Interesting," said Anne.

"What's interesting?"

"So, you deny it."

"I don't have the slightest idea what you're talking about."

"Julia, we've been friends since we were five years old. Did you really think you could keep something like this from me?"

"It doesn't make any difference, Anne. He is not the least bit interested in me, so you can let it lie, alright."

"I won't say another word about it. I only wanted you to admit it to me since I'm your best friend."

They sat there in the porch swing, silently rocking back and forth, for several minutes before either of them spoke again. It was

Anne. She said, "Nate certainly has problems these days, doesn't he? Everyone's talking about him."

"Yes," said Julia abstractedly.

"I heard Father talking to some men about it. They don't know why he paid so much for Yellowbush Flat. Everyone seems to think it has something to do with the railroad, but it won't do him a bit of good unless Lorna Fergin lets the road cross her land, and there's not much chance of that happening. Everyone thinks Nate is going to go broke and lose everything."

"Does everything include his ranch?" asked Julia, concerned for Tennet.

"I think everything means everything."

CHAPTER 11

When the train pulled into the siding, the big wagon, with its six horses standing patiently in the hot sun, had been there for nearly an hour. A single flatcar was decoupled and left at the siding, and the train went on its way. The flatcar held a steam boiler, a steam-powered compressor, some air hose—coiled and tied—two rock drills, and miscellaneous spare parts and accessories, all of which had been purchased from a mining company that had gone bust.

The waiting wagon was a converted ore hauler, with its high sides removed for this purpose. The flatbed had been reinforced, the axles had been greased, the wheels checked, and the brake blocks replaced. Nate Tennet and the two miners he had hired, Tom Howard and Luis Garza, were ready for their cargo. Virgil Trapp had been left with the ranch duties.

The unloading of the big boiler went well. The boiler was secured with chains, and Tennet climbed up and took the reins. The horses, ready for a change of circumstance, put their shoulders against the yokes, and the boiler began its short ride to Yellowbush Flat.

Later that day, the big compressor took the same ride, and within two days, the entire setup was ready for use. The boiler was on the ground, sitting on a wide, and very sturdy, wooden skid, to which it was securely bolted. The compressor was still on the wagon, where it would remain bolted to the reinforced bed.

Within two days of the unloading, the steam pipes and air hoses were all hooked up and the rock drills connected. The setup was ready for a test. It was all used equipment, but Tennet had been assured in the telegrams and letters through which he had corresponded with the representatives of the failed mining company that it was all functional and in good shape.

Tom Howard shoveled the coal into the boiler's firebox and started the fire. Luis Garza watched the needle on the pressure gauge and opened the steam valve at the appropriate time, sending pressurized steam to the compressor. The compressor's two flywheels began spinning, and soon the air pressure gauge began registering. Meanwhile, Howard went to one of the pneumatic rock drills, picked it up, rested its new tip on the ground, and waited.

For a time, Garza watched the needle on the air-pressure gauge slowly rise, and no one spoke. He was about to open the valve to send air to Howard's drill, when there was a clattering sound from the compressor.

Garza sprang down from the wagon bed and ran to the boiler, grasping the handle on the steam valve and shutting off the steam to the compressor, diverting it to the relief valve. He ran to the wagon and climbed back up to begin an inspection of the compressor. It wasn't long before he turned to Tennet, who was standing next to him, and said, "Bad crosshead bearing."

Tennet swore. He went to his horse and took a pencil and paper from the saddlebag. He wrote two different messages and gave them to Howard, saying, "Take these to the telegraph office. Tell Henry to send them right away."

It took nearly a week for the crosshead bearing to arrive, and a couple of hours to install it. The second test of the equipment was a success, and for the rest of the day, Garza and Howard drilled holes in the rock. That afternoon, Tennet came, driving a spring wagon. The two miners understood why he was driving slowly and cautiously, trying to avoid bumps and holes in the trail.

He was bringing the dynamite.

It was late in the afternoon when the ground shook, and windows in town rattled from the boom of an explosion. Priscilla was in her house, writing another letter to her most recent suitor, Mr. Anderson. She was replying in the affirmative to his request that she come to meet him. Hearing the noise, she jumped up and ran outside, where Jack and all the other people on the ranch were looking at the cloud of dust and smoke rising in the eastern sky.

"What was it?" she demanded of her brother.

"I don't know. Some kind of blast."

"Could that be Yellowbush Flat?" she asked.

"It's the right direction."

"Saddle me a horse."

"You don't give me orders, remember, Priscilla? We're partners."

She looked around in alarm, but no one else was near enough to have heard. She turned a murderous look on him, and hissed in a high whisper, "Why don't you just tell everyone my real name? Is there any way you could control your stupid mouth?" Then, raising her voice, she said, "Now saddle me a horse!"

Stull, red-faced and sullen, turned and stalked to the corral.

Forty minutes later, Priscilla was standing on a hilltop, looking across at the ridge where the explosion had taken place. The broken rock was scattered across the area, and the huge scar it had left on the face of the ridge was visible in the fading light. She saw the men, the compressor, and the boiler. She saw the snake-like compressor hoses, and it took her no time at all to realize what Tennet was doing. He intended to blast that ridge out of existence, and then build a road through the narrow valley in the hill and across the low, rolling flatlands beyond.

It was a perfect plan, and Priscilla instantly knew it. She cursed herself for not having thought of it, and she cursed Nate Tennet for having done so. Where was he getting all this money? Who was backing him?

The men below had set up a camp at the work site, and were now cooking their supper over the campfire, their day of labor finished. She rightly assumed Tennet had supplied them with rifles so they could protect his equipment from anyone who may desire to stop the work from proceeding.

For just a moment, Priscilla felt beaten. She felt the disappointment, the anger, the sense of loss. And she felt a sense of self-loathing at having allowed herself to be beaten. She had never felt these feelings before. She had always won her battles, often by killing those who got in her way, her stepmother having been the first of her victims.

What she did then would have been laudable in a person whose goals were lofty in nature, but Priscilla's purposes had always been selfish and malignant. She shrugged off her disappointment and discouragement, and made herself a commitment to thwart Nate Tennet in this new endeavor of his, in whatever way possible. She had invested far too much money in this deal to allow one man to beat her.

The following day, Jack Stull lay on his belly and watched through field glasses as Tennet's men below moved the rubble from the blasting of the previous day. Many of the pieces were too large to be moved by hand, and some of these they moved using chains and mules. There were a few chunks, however, that were too large even to be moved by this method, and in these, they were drilling holes with the clear intention of breaking them up with dynamite.

In addition to his two experienced miners, Tennet had, this morning, brought in ten laborers with pry bars, picks, shovels, and wheelbarrows. The work was progressing well, but Stull could see that it would take several weeks to completely demolish the ridge and move it out of the way. Still, it would be worth it, he knew. The railroad would pay well for the right-of-way across Tennet's land, and they would then be able to lay the tracks directly past the town, instead of several miles away, as Priscilla would have had it.

Stull cared nothing for the town or its inhabitants. His fortunes rested on his sister. If she succeeded, he would profit greatly. If she failed, he gained nothing. They had discussed it the night before, talking well into the night, and had made their plan. In keeping with that plan, Priscilla had left on the morning train, off to meet her next husband, and Jack Stull was on this hillside, aiming his rifle toward the men and equipment below.

He fired his first shot at the boiler and heard the ring of the metal as it hit. There was, however, no sound of escaping steam. It was as he had feared: the lead bullets in his rifle couldn't pierce the thick iron walls of the pressure vessel—at least, not from this distance.

He took aim at the air hose to one of the rock hammers and fired. The first shot missed, but the second scored, and from where he lay, Stull could hear the hiss of escaping air. The men below were scurrying like ants, all seeking cover. One of the miners had the presence of mind to run and turn off the air valve to the ruptured air hose, and then he also disappeared behind a boulder.

Stull fired a few more shots at different pieces of equipment, and was about to reload when a flurry of bullets started cutting up the dirt in front of him. Someone had spotted his position. He slid backward, down the hillside, and ran for his horse.

Nate Tennet ran for a rifle when the first shot came, but, not knowing the exact location of the shooter, he refrained from firing. Finally, after several shots, he was able to pick out the man's position and began sending bullets his way. When the shooting ceased, Tennet figured the shooter had gone. He ran to his horse, hoping to catch the man. Because of the terrain, it took him more than a half hour to get to the spot from where Stull had been shooting. All he found there were some tracks and some shell casings.

Because Priscilla had fired her foreman, there was no one to run the ranch while she was gone. She was reluctant to do so, but she told the crew she was putting Jack Stull in charge during her absence.

Stull was pleased. He had heretofore felt ignored, as though he was viewed as being of no importance. Now, in his sister's absence, he reveled in his authority, giving constant orders, even to the point of telling men to do tasks they were already doing. The men detested him.

One man, Ervin Green, fed up with Stull's abuse of authority, had the temerity to voice his opinion of Stull. The next morning found Green lying flat on the top of the hill where Jack Stull had lain only two mornings before. The hill was the one that afforded the best view of the area where Tennet's men were working. It was not, however, the highest hill in the area. There was another one that was higher, and, while not affording a good view of the work area, it did provide an excellent view of the very spot where Green now lay, planning to wreak havoc with Nate Tennet's crew and equipment.

Tennet was watching Green from the higher hill, and as the man prepared to fire his rifle, Tennet fired his, intentionally putting the bullet in the dirt next to Green. He shouted, "Drop the rifle."

Green rolled onto his side and, without taking time to aim, fired a quick shot at Tennet. His shot missed, and Tennet fired again, hitting him in the thigh. Green cried out and rolled onto his back.

Tennet ran down the hill to his horse, and rode to the place where Green had left his own mount. He waited there. When Green came, he was using his rifle as a crutch. Seeing Tennet, he reached for his pistol, but, because of the awkwardness of his position and the fact that he could bear no weight on his wounded leg, he fell sideways before he could get his gun out of the holster.

He lay on the ground, cursing Tennet, still trying to get his pistol out. Tennet ran over and kicked him in his wounded leg, and Green howled in pain.

Tennet said, "Do you want some more of that? Make another try for that gun, and I'll stand on that leg and do a dance."

Green finally grew calmer. It was clear that he was in pain, however, and after disarming him, Tennet tore off the man's shirt and used it to bandage the leg. Afterward, he helped Green onto his horse and said, "Tell Lorna Fergin the next man she sends will come back hangin' over the saddle, not sittin' in it."

Green appeared to be unable to think of anything appropriate to say, so he snarled a few curse words, and ended with, "Tell her yourself."

When the Lazy 8 man was gone, Tennet went back to his horse and rode to the work site. As he rode, he thought about the kind of men who worked for the Lazy 8. Saul Fergin had been that kind of man, and he had attracted and hired men of his own caliber. It appeared to Tennet that Saul had attracted a woman of his own caliber as well, but as he thought about it, Tennet decided that, if anything, Lorna was worse than Saul had ever been.

He wondered just how much worse she was, and it occurred to him that before this was all over, he might well find out.

Priscilla had been extremely uncomfortable with the idea of leaving her brother in charge of the ranch, but she needed money, and the only way she could think of to get it was by pushing ahead with the marriage to Mr. Anderson.

She stepped down from the train car, acting delicate and shy. Mr. Anderson was easy to spot; he was the eager-looking one with the bouquet of flowers.

The courtship was a short one. Priscilla, who was known to Mr. Anderson as Angela, used every trick she knew to stir his amorous feelings and make him think it was his own idea that they marry as soon as possible. Priscilla pretended to resist the suggestion of a hasty marriage, but finally, her desperate love for her dear Mr. Anderson—

the only man she had ever loved—together with his entreaties, overcame all caution in her. They were married by the pastor of Mr. Anderson's church, who was himself quite taken with Angela's demure, elegant nature, her quality of character, and her devotion to her Maker.

Angela told her new husband that she loved to take drives in the country. He was not averse to some fresh air himself, so each afternoon, he drove her far out into the pine-studded hills, coming back after being gone for hours.

Priscilla's circumstances were different this time than they had been with former victims. She needed to get back to the ranch. There was no time for a slow, lingering death for Mr. Anderson. She had been married to him for less than two weeks when, one evening, after not arriving back in town at their usual hour, causing some concern to their friends, the carriage came into town pulled by two lathered, exhausted horses, running breakneck speed, with Angela whipping them, screaming, sobbing, her hair flying.

Her dress was torn down the front, and the women of the town commented for weeks afterward that she would have had to be out of her head with fear and concern for her husband to allow herself to be seen that way by the men of the town. They all agreed that she was in such a state that she was completely unaware of the revealing condition of her clothes.

To the men, she was an instant heroine. To have made that long ride, driving the horses the way she had, ignoring all other considerations, even that of feminine modesty, was the noblest of acts, and many a hardened masculine eye became moist while speaking of it.

Mr. Anderson was dead, shot in the heart by a road agent, who was, sadly, never apprehended. To be fair, the posse had very little information to guide them. Mrs. Anderson was so emotionally overwrought by the experience that she had, according to the doctor, a mild form of amnesia. She remembered the event—the robbery and the shooting of her husband, the attack on her person which she had, thankfully, been able to fight off using her husband's buggy whip—but she recalled very little else. She did not recall the location of the crime, nor could she describe the road agent or his horse. All she knew—or cared about—was that her beloved Mr. Anderson was dead. She had never loved another man and never would again.

Priscilla left the life of Angela Anderson behind and returned to that of Lorna Fergin, a far richer woman than she had been just a few weeks ago. It would take some time for the affairs of the estate to be settled, and she had left it in the hands of a trusted lawyer, one of Mr. Anderson's personal friends, instructing him to correspond with her family lawyer in Chicago, the man who, she said, took care of her meager finances. She took with her, however, a substantial sum that was granted to her for living expenses, some of which she sent to Deborah Pence of the Matrimonial Correspondence Club.

When she returned, she found the affairs of the ranch in complete disarray. Some of the men had quit, others refused to obey Jack Stull's orders unless forced to do so on threat of being shot. She also learned that Stull had been unable to halt or even slow down Nate Tennet's crew of rock breakers, as they were being called in town. Tennet had hired two sharpshooters to sit on hilltops in the area and guard the laborers. He had sent the wounded Ervin Green back to the Lazy 8, warning against further interference. On the whole, things had fallen apart in Priscilla's absence.

She gave her brother the expected tongue lashing, after which he said, "I'm going to live over at the Rupp place. You need me, you can come over there. All you've got here is a bunch of whining pansies, anyhow. This ain't a ranch; it's a nursery." He stormed out and rode to town to get drunk. The next day, he took his war bag over to the Rupp place, which was being used as a line shack, and made it his home, wondering why he hadn't thought of this before.

After Jack left, Priscilla began going through her accumulated mail. In it, there was a letter from Deborah Pence. Priscilla's payment to Deborah and this letter must have passed each other in the mail.

The letter was an interesting one, and she read it three times. Was it too soon, she wondered, to get married again?

CHAPTER 12

Marshal Pitts brought sandwiches and milk, and the three men began eating. Sutherton had no aversion to talking while he ate, so he continued his story. "It was an interesting state of affairs indeed, gentlemen. I was playing nursemaid to the two boys, and nurse to Dale Ramsey. And I was supposed to be retired. Kyle and Willie were now living on my property, milking my cow, and taking half the milk as their pay, which, I don't mind telling you, was a good bargain for me. Owning a cow is like being married. It's another form of slavery." Then, he looked at the marshal and asked, "Are you married?"

The marshal started to reply, but the judge spoke first—in a mildly offended tone. "I'm a widower, sir, but I look upon the matrimonial state as a blessed one."

The marshal said, "I'm married. We'll leave it at that."

"No offense intended to the institution of marriage," said Sutherton, inclining his head toward the judge.

"None taken," said the judge, inclining his in reply.

Sutherton said, "We'll defer any talk of marriage for later. Suffice it to say, a cow is a demanding critter. She has to be milked every morning without fail and every night without fail. You can't go away for a week and milk her fourteen times when you get back. No, it's two times every day."

He bit into a sandwich and chewed for a few moments, then said, "I let the boys gather my eggs and keep half of them for themselves. I let Kyle slaughter a hog and keep half. I let them help take care of Ramsey, too. I would have given them all of him, but it wouldn't work. I paid them a little for helping me with him, and they were glad to have it. It worked out for all of us."

He took a long drink of milk, wiped his mouth with his handkerchief, and said, "One day, I began thinking about the strange circumstances of old Saul Fergin's marriage and death. Seemed mighty odd that he would be as healthy as a horse all his life, then he gets married and takes sick, goes downhill, and finally dies, leaving the little lady with everything he has built in a lifetime of work. While I was thinking about it, I recalled a similar situation I had heard about back in Missouri not long before. I wrote a letter to someone I knew back there, asking some specific questions. When I received my reply, it made me even more curious, so I wrote letters to people in several different states, asking them if they would inquire in the appropriate quarters and get back to me.

"It took weeks, but the letters trickled in, one by one, and they told an interesting story."

Sutherton took another bite of his sandwich and leaned back in the chair, extending his legs and stretching his arms over his head. He swallowed the food and took a drink of milk. "You wouldn't think that talking would make a man so tired." He yawned.

Trying not to act too interested, Judge Markham said, "What story?"

"Hmm?"

"The story, the story the letters told. You said they told an interesting story."

"Oh. Yes, that story. Yes, it was more than interesting. It was fascinating, and horrifying at the same time."

After another pause, the judge said, "Well, tell it, man, tell the story."

Sutherton's expression grew suddenly sober. He leaned forward and said, "This murderous woman, whoever she was, somehow found well-off men who were looking for a wife. She would write to them, playing the part of whatever kind of woman they were looking for, and they would marry her. In all cases but one, the husband later became mysteriously ill and slowly grew worse until he died."

"Sounds like poisoning to me," said Judge Markham.

The marshal was nodding his head in agreement. He said, "You said in all cases but one. What was the one?"

"It was the most recent one. Up in Wyoming. A wealthy widower corresponded with a lady, who seemed to be just the kind of wife he was seeking. They decided to meet, and despite the fact that he was much older than her, and far from handsome, she soon professed to be deeply in love with him. They got married right away."

Judge Markham was frowning. He said, "I don't see what a man's looks or a difference in age have to do with love. If two people are attracted to each other, say, in the spiritual sense, those things shouldn't make a bit of difference."

"I didn't say they did, Your Honor."

"Well, you certainly implied it."

"Objection sustained, sir. My apology. The jury will disregard that statement."

Mollified, the judge gave a sheepish smile, and said, "Carry on, sir."

Sutherton said, "The newlyweds, were, by all appearances, very happy. They had the custom of going for long drives in the country in an open carriage. One day, the wife drove the carriage back to town on the run, with her dear husband in the seat beside her, dead from a gunshot wound in the chest. She claimed they had been accosted by a robber. The robber was never apprehended."

Neither Sutherton's expression nor his voice gave any indication as to whether or not he believed the wife's story. He looked back and forth at the faces of his two listeners for a moment, then continued. "In all these cases, the widow inherited substantial value, in cash and property. In every case, but one, she retained a local lawyer to handle the affairs of probate and the liquidation of the assets, and to correspond with her attorney in Chicago, who would handle the details on her end. And . . . in every case but one, she left the area, never to return."

Before either of his listeners could ask the question, Sutherton explained, "The exception is the case of the aging rancher, near my current home, who married a young woman and shortly thereafter became ill. He died a few months later. The widow, in this case, did not leave immediately, but stayed around to run the ranch."

"What makes you think it was the same woman in all these cases?" asked the marshal.

"In my inquiries, I asked for detailed physical descriptions of the woman. In every case, the descriptions in the replies I received matched each other perfectly. But there's more, gentlemen, much more."

Try as she might, Priscilla was unable to find a way to thwart Nate Tennant in his dismantling of the ridge. His sharpshooters were there to keep anyone from climbing a hill and shooting at men or equipment. She hired a half-breed Indian to sneak into the camp at night and damage the equipment, but the most he was able to do was cut some of the air hoses, and these, Tennet's men repaired in a couple of hours.

She thought of sending her men to do an all-out raid on the camp and kill everyone there, but quickly discarded the idea. Even if her men were willing to comply with that order, which she very much doubted, such a crime would be easily traced back to her. She remembered when the sheriff had come around, questioning her and her men about the burning of Tennet's barns and the killing of Doug Connors. Like everyone else in the valley, the sheriff had known the crimes were committed by the Lazy 8, but he lacked any real evidence. After that, Priscilla had decided to be more careful. The last thing she wanted was to wind up in jail, or on the gallows.

Still, she was determined to beat Nate Tennet one way or another. She remembered, with enormous bitterness, how he had humiliated her that night under the tree. She would never forget it— nor forgive. If she could not have the right-of-way into town, she would make sure Tennet did not have it, either. She had already sent a letter to Nestor Bradley, explaining the situation and telling him they would need to alter their plan. Bradley had sent back a telegram, agreeing with her and telling her he would file the revised document with his company.

As long as the railroad didn't go through the canyon behind the ridge that Tennet and his crew were currently demolishing, it would still have to take the route she and Nestor Bradley had laid out: one that, though it bypassed the town, would still cross a large section of the Lazy 8 and several other pieces of land owned by Priscilla. She would love to see Tennet's face when he learned that all his work and all the money he had spent on Yellowbush Flat, on the rock drilling equipment, and on paying the workers, was wasted.

Ruining Tennet financially would be incredibly satisfying. Priscilla would watch as he lost everything and ended up completely bankrupt. And after he had suffered all those things—all the worry, pain, loss and humiliation—when she decided he had suffered enough, she would send Jack Stull to kill him.

The work progressed more rapidly than Tennet had anticipated, and within a few weeks, the ridge had been broken up and most of the larger pieces of it moved to the side. All that remained now was the removal of a few tons of smaller rubble. The railroad could do the rest; they would only be purchasing a right-of-way, not a graded road.

Tennet stood gazing at the notch in the hill that had formerly been obstructed by the ridge, and at the low hills and flatlands beyond, and could easily visualize the stretch of tracks that would be laid there. It was all his land. Everything from here at Yellowbush Flat almost all the way to town belonged to him.

He had had no more trouble from the Lazy 8, and had dismissed all but one of the sharpshooters. He did not, however, delude himself that Lorna Fergin was finished with him. He had no idea what her next move would be, but he knew he had better be wary and cautious.

When the railroad representative showed up, he was a week late, and he was the wrong man. He had been in the valley for two days when Jack Stull first heard about it through a casual comment made in a saloon. Stull rode back to the Lazy 8 as fast as he could.

Priscilla had not sent for Jack since their falling out. He had lived at the Rupp farm, sharing the place with Trey Paxton, one of the Lazy 8 hands who was there with orders to make sure no one—particularly the Rupp boys—were allowed onto the property. Paxton was a malcontent, and he was disliked by nearly everyone on the ranch. He was surly and easily offended, and when he took offense, he often tried to push the offending party into a gunfight. Priscilla had been killing two birds with one stone when she sent him to stay at the Rupp farm. She had gotten the man off the ranch and away from the other men, and he was ideal for the job of watchdog at the farm.

She was in her office when Stull arrived. He stepped in, unannounced, and sat down. She looked at him coldly, and said, "Soon I'll be selling this place and moving on. As I recall, we agreed on a third for you."

"I thought it was half." Stull was more than half joking. He knew she wouldn't forget their deal.

"Don't try to play games with me, Jack. You should know by now it doesn't work."

"Here's a game you'll have to play, Pris. I know something you don't. And you really need to know it."

"What is it?"

"Guess."

She picked up a book from the desk and hurled it at him. "Tell me," she barked.

He told her.

"Two days?" she said in alarm. "What's he been doing?"

"From what I hear, he's been out gettin' the lay of the land for the railroad spur."

Priscilla's tone was furious. "What? That's what he was going to let us show *him*. What's gotten into Bradley?"

Stull was afraid of no man, but at this moment, he dreaded saying what he was about to say to his sister. "Well, that's the worst news of all. It ain't Nestor Bradley. It's some other owl hoot."

As Stull had expected, Priscilla ranted for a few moments, finally growing calmer until she was able to say, "Let's go find this 'owl hoot', and talk to him."

Stull told Priscilla the man was named James Harper, and he had taken a room in the hotel. When they got to town, Stull went to the man's room and knocked on the door. When the door was opened, Stull told the man he represented the Lazy 8 ranch, and the owner was downstairs and would like to speak with him.

Priscilla was her most charming self. She had dressed for the occasion, and when the railroad representative offered to shake her hand, she took it in her two small, soft hands and held it as if they were old friends, looking in his eyes and saying, "It's so nice to meet you, Mr. Harper. It's so seldom that we get visitors of such distinction."

"Thank you," he said. "The name's actually Harker."

Priscilla's eyes shot a quick, accusatory dart at Jack, and she apologized to Harker.

"No matter, happens all the time," he said. "Now, what can I do for you?"

Priscilla motioned him to a chair and said, "Can we sit down?"

"Certainly."

She produced a small, ribbon-wrapped bundle of cigars and held it out to him. "My late husband left these, and I have no use for such things. I'm told they are of excellent quality."

"Thank you, I neither smoke nor drink."

"A man after my own heart. I dislike all such vices," said Priscilla, recovering quickly and setting the cigars on the table beside her chair.

Mr. Harker repeated his question, "What can I do for you?"

Priscilla said, "Over the past few months, I have had several meetings with Mr. Nestor Bradley, regarding the route of the spur your company proposes to build here. We had agreed—"

Harker interrupted, "Then I find myself in the position of being the bearer of bad news. Mr. Bradley has died."

Priscilla's shock was unfeigned. "Died? How?"

Harker said, "I knew Nestor for over fifteen years, and for most of that time he was, to put it bluntly, a drunkard. But, a few years ago he gave up the bottle and was dry for a number of years. Then, just recently, for some reason, he took it up again. Last month, he was in a saloon, quite drunk, and he got into an altercation with a fellow drinker. There were fisticuffs, and Nestor lost, fell down, and went unconscious. They took him home, where he died three days later. The doctor said it was apoplexy. All because of alcohol."

There was a long silence, as Priscilla wrestled with her disappointment and her anger toward Stull, who had been the catalyst in Nestor Bradley's resumption of his drunken habits. During this silence, Stull carefully avoided looking at Priscilla.

Apparently misinterpreting the silence, Harker said, "I'm sorry. Were you close friends?"

"Yes, quite close," said Priscilla, dabbing at her eyes with a handkerchief, though they were perfectly dry. Then she said, "I hope we can honor Nestor's memory by carrying through with the agreement that he and I made. I know it would mean a lot to him."

Harker folded his arms on his chest. "What agreement would that be?"

Priscilla produced and unfolded a piece of paper, on which was drawn an intricate map of the area, including her proposed route for the railroad spur. She had changed the map in the manner she and Nestor Bradley had agreed upon, so that it bypassed Tennet's land—

and the town—and crossed her ranch on its way north, where it would also cross other pieces of land owned by her. She showed the map to Harker, pointing out different landmarks and explaining all the reasons why the tracks had to follow the route shown on the drawing.

Harker said, "Mrs. Fergin, this map is out of date."

"What exactly do you mean, sir? It was drawn quite recently."

"Not recently enough, I'm afraid. It fails to show that at this spot right here," he pointed to the spot on the map, "there is an opening through the hills, that until recently was blocked by a ridge."

Priscilla started to speak in her most ingratiating tone. "Mr. Harker, I think if we, you and I—"

Harker interrupted her, "Forgive me, Mrs. Fergin, but the decision has already been made. In fact, the papers were signed yesterday. I have purchased the right-of-way from a Mr. Tennet. Do you know him?"

CHAPTER 13

For some time, Kyle had been worried about Willie. The boy was not adjusting to their new life at all. He talked constantly about home, reminding Kyle of his promise that they would soon be going back there. He was not eating well, and Kyle was worried about his brother's health.

Kyle regretted having told Willie they would be going back home soon. He had done it to calm and reassure the boy, and at the time, he had been determined to make it a reality. He had since lost that hope. Now, Kyle knew, he needed to get a job and find a place for him and Willie to live. He would have done it before now, but his discouragement had robbed him of all motivation.

It was time for the evening milking. Kyle called to Willie, but received no response. He went looking for the boy, realizing it had been hours since he had seen him. Willie was nowhere to be found. Kyle went out to the pasture and counted the horses. Jumper, the old mare Willie rode, was gone. He ran to the barn and checked the saddle rack. Willie's saddle was gone.

Kyle hastily saddled his own horse, went for his pistol, and strapped it on. Spurring the horse on as fast as he dared, he rode toward the farm. He knew Willie would be going there. He only hoped he could catch the boy before he arrived.

Willie rode into the yard of what had, until recently, been his home all his life. It felt good to be back. He had no understanding of property deeds, or legal documents of any kind. In his anger, Kyle had told him the farm still rightfully belonged to them, and the people who now resided there had no right to it. Willie did not understand why, if those things were true, they could not go home and tell the men there to leave. He had grown tired of waiting for someone else to do that, and had decided to take matters into his own hands.

Jack Stull was not there, having ridden to town to spend some time in his favorite saloon, drinking and gambling. Trey Paxton was there, however, and, hearing the hoof beats of Willie's horse, he looked out the window. Seeing a stranger in the yard, he strapped on his pistol and came out onto the porch.

Willie said to him, "Go away from my house. You have to leave now."

Paxton laughed. "Who are you?"

"Willie Rupp. You go away."

Willie dismounted and led his horse to the barn, where he began removing the saddle. Paxton walked over and said, "Boy, you unsaddle that nag, and you'll leave here afoot. This ain't your place no more. Now climb back up on your fleabag and get out."

Willie pulled the saddle off and started carrying it to the barn. Paxton walked around him, grasped the saddle, and wrenched it from his hands, throwing it on the ground. He grasped Willie by the ear and held him up, kicking him, the boy's feet barely touching the ground.

Willie screamed and thrashed, trying to get loose. Laughing, Paxton let go of his ear and caught him by the hair. He gave the boy a vicious slap, and Willie fell to the ground and lay there, rolling his head, only partially conscious. Paxton reached down, grasped the boy by the front of his shirt, and hauled him to his feet.

There was a high-pitched scream of rage and the pounding of hooves, and Paxton dropped Willie and pulled his gun from the holster. He did not know who this was, but it could be nothing but an enemy.

Kyle had seen the scene before he entered the yard, and his rage and concern for his brother blotted out all other considerations. Now, seeing Paxton raise his pistol and aim it at him, Kyle recognized his danger. He jerked the reins and pulled the horse to the side, at the same time leaning low in the saddle, and when Paxton fired, he missed.

The maneuver had put Kyle behind the barn, out of the line of Paxton's sight. But it had also placed him in a blind alley. In front of him was the corral fence, and his old horse could not possibly jump it. He could climb over the fence himself and run, but he would be out in the open then, for as long as it took him to cross the wide pasture, and Paxton could shoot him at his pleasure. Moreover, there was Willie to think of. Kyle could not run away and leave his brother there.

He heard the sound of Paxton's boots as he ran toward him. There was only one thing to do. He threw himself out of the saddle and dropped to his hands and knees, pushing on a particular board at the base of the barn wall. He knew this board well and hoped no one had repaired it. It gave as he pushed it, and he crawled inside, moving the board back into position just as Paxton came around the corner of the barn.

Kyle sat in the dim interior of the barn, his heart pounding, trying to control his breathing. He peered through a crack between two boards, and saw the daylight obscured as Paxton passed.

His mind churned, trying to think of a way out of this predicament for him and Willie. He had not thought to pull his gun, but he did so now. He knew this man meant to kill him. It seemed unreal that he could be in this situation. He thought of Sutherton and asked himself what the man would do if he were in such circumstances, and it occurred to him that Sutherton would never have allowed himself to become trapped like this.

There was no need for all this. He and Willie posed no threat to this man. They could just go away and leave him alone; there was no reason for anyone to die today. He decided to talk to the man. He called out, "Mister, if you'll let me get my brother, I'll—"

The bullet crashed through the board just to the side of Kyle, and Kyle's heart jumped in alarm at the sound. He threw himself to one side just as another shot crashed, and a hole appeared in the wood in front of where he had been squatting moments before.

Kyle had the advantage of being able to place Paxton's position by the way the man's body blocked the light coming through the cracks, whereas Paxton could only guess at Kyle's position.

Kyle understood, now, that there would be no reasoning with this man. The man was determined to kill. To speak to him again would only bring more bullets. Kyle knew what he had to do, but the thought of killing was suddenly repulsive to him. He had never known it would be like this.

Another shot broke the silence and punctured the barn wall. Willie had come out of his daze, and now he began to cry. It was the sound of his brother's voice, the knowledge of his brother's danger, that made Kyle pull the trigger. He could not miss, he knew. The man was no more than three feet away from him. He heard Paxton grunt, heard him fall, saw through a crack Paxton's inert form on the ground.

Willie's crying was louder, and Kyle went out to comfort the boy. Seeing Kyle, Willie stopped crying and said, "Can we stay home now?"

Kyle dropped his head, emotion overcoming him. He was about to speak when he heard the sound of a horse entering the yard. He looked up and saw Jack Stull riding in.

Stull reined in about twenty feet away from Kyle and sat there, looking first at Paxton lying on the ground, then at Willie, and lastly at Kyle. Stull motioned to Paxton and said to Kyle, "Did you do that?"

Kyle nodded. He felt a knot in his stomach. His mouth was so dry, he was sure he would be unable to speak if he tried.

Stull grinned, "Looks like you're a big-time killin' man."

Kyle said nothing. He waited.

Stull's grin went away. He spat on the ground. "That man was a friend of mine," he lied.

Kyle managed to speak. "He was thrashin' my little brother."

"Your little brother deserved to be thrashed. You don't kill a man for that."

"He shot at me."

"Now, why would he do that? Ain't like a man would be afraid of the pair of you."

Kyle said nothing. He knew this man was playing with him. He was filled with dread. There was no possibility he could shoot this man as he had the other one.

Stull said, "Well, now that you're a gunslinger, let's see how good you are. I'll count to three, we'll both go for our guns, and we'll see who comes out second best."

He started to count. "One—"

"Stull!"

The single word rang out in the silence like a thunderclap.

Jack Stull stiffened. He knew better than to wheel around and possibly cause this newcomer to react in alarm. He turned slowly to face Earl Sutherton, who, like him, was sitting on a horse.

Stull inclined his head slightly. "Earl. Didn't expect to see you here."

Sutherton glanced pointedly at the two boys and said, "Don't guess you did."

"Friends of yours?" said Stull.

"Uh huh."

Stull went for his gun.

It was close. Very close. Stull's hammer was back, and the barrel was pointed at Sutherton when Sutherton's bullet passed through his heart and spine. Stull fell from his horse, landing headfirst on the ground and rolling onto his back.

Sutherton got down and checked the body afterward, going around to the side of the barn to check Trey Paxton's body. He came back and said to Kyle, "Something I never taught you. You shoot a man, you always check to make sure he's dead."

CHAPTER 14

"**S**o, Jack Stull is dead," said Marshal Pitts. Then he added, "No loss to the world."

"No," agreed Sutherton. "I reckon when I meet my Maker, and he asks me what good I did in the world, I can say, 'I took Jack Stull out of it.' Maybe that'll earn me a spot in the cooler side of hell."

Judge Markham chuckled. "Wouldn't doubt it, sir. Wouldn't doubt it at all."

Sutherton said, "The boys wanted to stay at their farm, but I suggested they wait a bit. Kyle was mighty shook up about killing a man, and the Lazy 8 was still a danger. I had heard about the way Nate Tennet had outfoxed Lorna Fergin and gotten the railroad to buy the right-of-way across his land instead of hers, and it looked to me like her plan was coming unraveled, so I told the boys to be patient just a little while longer.

"We put the two bodies in the bed of a buckboard, and I took them to town while the boys went back to my place to do the chores. I took the bodies to the sheriff and told him everything just like it had happened. He agreed it was self-defense, and he said nobody in the valley would care much that a couple of Lazy 8 hard cases had gotten killed, especially those two hard cases. He said he'd meet us at the Rupp farm in the morning, so he could talk to Kyle and look things over. He told me the man Kyle Rupp had killed was named Trey Paxton, and he was as bad as they come. He was always looking for a fight when he came to town, and people tried to avoid him. He was supposed to have had something of a reputation with a gun, too. I told him Kyle Rupp had killed him in a fair fight, and he said, 'I know Kyle. He's a fine boy, but I never figured him as being much of a hand with a gun.'

"I told him that Kyle had ridden in just as Paxton was giving Willie a pretty nasty thrashing. I said I had come along a little later, and the kid was still bleeding. He nodded and said, 'Kind of makes sense. Kyle was always real protective of that kid.'

"The sheriff's name was Benson," said Sutherton. "He knew who Jack Stull was, of course, and he said, 'Not just any man could beat Stull in a gunfight.' Implying he'd like to know more about my past. I said, 'Sheriff, would it bother you if I asked you to allow me to be who I am here in this place, and not who I was before I came here?' He smiled and said, 'I figure a man's past is in the past. We'll leave it at that.'"

Sutherton now looked at Marshal Pitts, and said, "Now, that's the kind of lawman I can respect."

Pitts looked noncommittally down at the floor, and Sutherton continued.

"Next morning, we met with the sheriff at the Rupp farm, and Kyle told him the story just like he had told it to me. The sheriff looked at the tracks, the blood stains on the ground, and the bullet holes in the barn wall—three going in and one going out—and said he didn't see any reason to disbelieve us. He shook our hands and rode away."

Marshal Pitts was nodding in unconscious approval of this other lawman's actions.

The judge said, "Good man, good man."

"Because of the nature of my former occupation," continued Sutherton, "you'll understand why I didn't have any lawmen as friends or personal acquaintances. But I knew people who did, and I sent letters and telegrams out to quite a number of them regarding what I had pieced together about the woman I knew as Lorna Fergin."

"Am I to take it you were completely convinced that it was the same woman in every one of those cases?" asked the judge.

"Completely, sir. But what I lacked was something that tied all the cases together. As I thought about it, I realized that what I didn't know was how the woman had learned about these men, their unmarried state, their financial circumstances, and their desire for a young wife. It seemed pretty clear to me that she had to have an accomplice. So, I sent out some more letters." He smiled. "Gentlemen, you'll never guess what I learned."

The two men waited, intensely interested in Sutherton's story, and intensely anxious to hear what he had learned.

But, Sutherton disappointed them. He said, "Ah, but I've left out some of the story."

"What did you learn?" asked the marshal.

"In a minute," replied Sutherton. "First, let me tell you the rest of the story about Dale Ramsey."

The marshal and the judge exchanged a quick glance of mutual disappointment, and the marshal gave a little shrug. Sutherton was in control, and they accepted it.

Sutherton said, "Ramsey healed up faster than I would have ever expected, but it did not improve his disposition in the least. Never have I seen a man who was more angry and bitter. He was filled with hatred. He told me the story about getting fired by Lorna Fergin, and getting shot by Jack Stull, none of which was helpful to me in any way. But he did tell me something else that was quite interesting."

"What was that?" asked Judge Markham.

"Just be patient, gents. The story will be more interesting if you hear it in the proper order of events. Anyhow, it was bad enough that a man like myself, who loves his solitude, now had a sick man and two orphans staying with him. Yes, you guessed it, gentlemen: I had softened to the point of letting the boys stay inside the house, instead of just camping on my property."

Sutherton shook his head as though disgusted with himself, but he had a faint smile on his lips. "Like I was saying, it was bad enough having all that company, but living under the same roof with Ramsey was just about unbearable. The man did nothing but complain and whine about everything. You'd have thought he was paying me, the way he groused about the food, the noise Willie made, and just about anything else he could think of. But, his main topic of conversation was his hatred of Jack Stull and Lorna Fergin. I didn't tell him Jack Stull was dead. I didn't know if he would be pleased or angry about it, but I'll tell you, gents, the day Dale Ramsey decided he was ready to leave—and did it—was a happy day for me and those two boys.

"I knew that the sale of the Rupp farm to the Lazy 8 had been completely illegal. Jack Stull had coerced Kyle Rupp into signing over the deed, and I was convinced the court would rule in favor of the boys. But the time was not right for that. It would come soon enough, I was sure. Meanwhile, it turned out that Kyle was, like myself, a reader, and we had read many of the same books. It was pleasant to sit around in the evenings and talk to someone who had some things in common with me. I had always thought my dogs and my books were all the companionship I needed, but . . ."

He paused and grinned. "You've heard what Mark Twain said about that, haven't you, gents?"

The marshal shook his head.

The judge said, "Can't say as I have."

Sutherton chuckled. "Mr. Twain said, 'Outside of a dog, a book is a man's best friend. Inside of a dog, it's too dark to read.'"

The three men had a good laugh together, and the judge said, "That's one of the best ones I've heard in a long time."

"Me too," said Marshal Pitts.

Priscilla shed no tears for her brother. She had been trying to think of a way to keep from giving him his promised third of the take from this deal, and now she wouldn't have to.

She had lost out on the railroad deal, and there was no changing that. There was no further reason to stay around. She contacted an attorney in town to handle the sale of the ranch and the Rupp farm, and made her arrangements to go meet the latest wealthy gentleman, whose name had been given to her by Deborah Pence. She felt she had stayed too long in this place and was anxious to leave as soon as possible. Soon, Lorna Fergin would cease to exist.

Nate Tennet was in town, buying supplies. He had taken on two more hands as well as a cook, and was buying a lot more food than in the past. The money from the sale of the right-of-way to the railroad was in the bank, minus the amount he had used to pay back John Longhurst. He had contacted a mining company in Utah about selling them his compressor and boiler and rock drills, and had received a letter stating their interest. Things were going well.

He had seen Julia and her father about twenty minutes ago in the restaurant, and he and Longhurst had spoken as the friends they were. Julia had, as usual, seemed distant.

Now, as he brought his supplies out the back door of the store, loading them into the spring wagon, he saw Julia come around the corner, walking in haste. Perplexed, he watched as she came toward him. He watched for a smile, hoped for a smile, but her countenance was grave.

She stopped in front of him and said without preamble, "Dale Ramsey's over in Ballenger's, talking mean. Says he wants to see you."

"I thought he was gone from these parts," said Tennet.

"Everyone did, but he rode in today and started talking about how he was going to kill Jack Stull. They say he acted disappointed when he found out Stull was already dead."

Tennet laughed. "He's the only one. I'll bet even Stull's mama didn't cry when he died."

"How can you joke about this? Don't you know he'll be coming for you?"

Tennet shrugged. "It's a free country, Julia."

"Oh, I hate you sometimes, Nate. What if—?"

"I thought you hated me all the time," he said bitterly, turning away.

She grasped his shirt sleeve and pulled him back around. "You fool. Don't you understand? What if he kills you?"

Tennet gazed at her in perplexity for a moment. He said, "You act like it matters to you."

She was angry, now. "Why should it matter to me if it doesn't to you?"

Suddenly, he realized this last statement had nothing to do with the possibility of him dying. He looked at her in wonderment, wanting to be sure. She stood there in front of him, her face turned up to look at him, her eyes wet, her lips beckoning.

He pulled her to him and kissed her, and she was giving and warm. They did not pull apart for what seemed like a very long time.

Tennet heard Ramsey's voice shouting from the street. Shouting his name. John Longhurst came around the corner and said to Julia, "There you are." He looked at her face and then at Tennet's and murmured, "About time." He spoke to Tennet, his voice grave. "I'll side you, Nate."

"Thanks, no need."

"Will anyway."

Tennet pulled away from Julia. She started to call after him, but her father said, "Not your place, girl." He followed Tennet.

Seeing that Ramsey was alone, John Longhurst stayed on the boardwalk as Tennet walked out into the middle of the street. Tennet loosened his pistol in its holster and moved his hand away from it. He shouted after Ramsey, who was walking away from him. "Ramsey!"

Ramsey spun around. Seeing Tennet, he smiled. He walked toward Tennet and said, "Heard you were in town. Didn't think you'd run. You're like me. We like to see things finished."

"We don't have to finish them this way, Dale. The world's a big place. You should've just ridden away."

Ramsey smiled. "No, Nate. No matter where a man goes, he's got to live with himself. Jack Stull is dead, you know."

It took Tennet a moment to grasp what Ramsey was saying, and then he did. He said, "You've been laid up, haven't you?"

"Knew you'd figure it out. I tried to throw down on Stull, but he was faster."

Tennet understood. It was all about Ramsey's pride. Stull had beaten him, and if Stull were still alive, Ramsey would have had no need to fight Tennet. But Stull was dead.

Tennet said, "You're a fool, Dale."

"We're all fools, Nate, and sooner or later, we all die from it."

It was all in an instant. Ramsey drew his gun. Tennet pulled his and sidestepped to the left as he did. No one ever knew who fired first. Ramsey's bullet passed between Tennet's right arm and the side of his ribcage, taking a small chunk of flesh off the inside of his arm.

Tennet's bullet hit Ramsey in the middle of his torso, doubling him over and knocking him backward. Tennet walked over to him, and Ramsey wheezed, "It's all right, Nate. Everything's . . ." And he was dead.

CHAPTER 15

Sutherton pulled out his watch, looked at it, and said, "It's getting late, gentlemen. I'll try to wind it up, now, so you can go home and get some sleep." He looked at the marshal. "Won't your wife be getting worried about you?"

"No. She's used to my hours. She usually don't even wake up when I slip into bed."

Sutherton did not look at the judge. He started on the story again. "Gentlemen, at that point, I was writing so many letters, and receiving so many replies, that I was afraid I was going to overload the postal service. I rode to town every day and opened my mail on the boardwalk right outside the post office. I always carried paper, and I would use the pen and ink in the lobby of the hotel to answer my correspondences. When I was finished, which sometimes took hours, I would take those letters directly to the post office before I rode home. I have to tell you, gents, I was truly enjoying myself. I was putting together a strong case against this woman, whoever she was—and that was the problem. I still didn't know her real name. Then, one day I remembered something Dale Ramsey—rest his black soul—had said to me. He said he thought Jack Stull and Lorna Fergin looked a lot alike, like maybe they were brother and sister. That got me thinking, so I started an investigation into Stull's background, which led me to learn that he had a sister, and she was the right age. It also turned up some interesting information about the death of their stepmother, and I'll tell you about that later.

"During this whole time, gentlemen, the amount of mail coming to my town increased substantially because of me, and I can tell you the postmaster was mighty curious about it all. He must have been talking around town, because, suddenly, I was being treated like somebody important—due partly, I can only assume, to the number of letters and telegrams I was receiving, and partly to the fact that many of them were from law-enforcement people. My status in town had become so favorable that when I approached the local authorities about getting the Rupp farm back for its rightful owners, and produced the affidavit written and signed by Kyle Rupp, describing the coercion Jack Stull had used to steal the farm from them, there was no hesitation at all. The judge ruled in favor of the Rupp boys."

"As I would have," said Judge Markham.

Sutherton smiled and said, "And, speaking of the Rupps, Kyle's standing in the community had been helped considerably by the fact that he had killed Trey Paxton in a gunfight."

Marshal Pitts chuckled. "There's nothin' like killin' a public nuisance to make folks appreciate a man."

"True," said Sutherton. "The day after the boys went back to live at their own place, Kyle paid me a visit to ask my advice on a particular matter that was troubling him. He said he and Willie had found a substantial sum of money in their house. He figured it must have belonged to Jack Stull. He said, 'I don't know what to do with it. It ain't our money, so it doesn't seem right to keep it. I just don't know who to give it to.'

"I said, 'Well, Kyle, it looks like old Jack Stull wasn't such a bad fellow after all.'

"'What do you mean?' he asked me.

"'He just paid his back rent.'

The judge and the marshal were both smiling, nodding in agreement with Sutherton's handling of the matter. Judge Markham said, "The wisdom of Solomon, sir. I applaud you."

Sutherton gave the judge a faint, respectful bow of the head, then he was pensive for a moment as he looked directly at the judge. Presently, he looked away and said, "But, none of that matters here, gentlemen. What does matter is that I found out how the woman was getting connected with her victims."

He paused again, his face grave. Up to this point, he had appeared to be enjoying himself, but now he seemed reluctant to proceed. Finally, soberly, he said, "All the victims had been referred to the woman by an agency called the Matrimonial Correspondence Club, located in Chicago, Illinois."

He stopped speaking. There was silence in the room.

Judge Markham's face had gone pale. He stared at Sutherton, his eyes wide, his mouth partially open. Marshal Pitts was looking back and forth between the judge and Sutherton, clearly not comprehending.

The silence stretched out until, at last, the judge said, "You knew."

"Yes."

It took a moment, but the judge seemed to regain his mental equilibrium. He said, "Sir, I have listened to your story with interest, and I don't doubt that you have accumulated some information regarding these deaths, but if you are implying that my Molly is the same woman who killed those men, why . . . all I can say is it's preposterous. It's not possible. Molly is the kindest, sweetest, most generous woman . . . it's not possible."

Sutherton looked down at the floor. He did not speak.

Judge Markham persisted. "Surely, this woman you speak of is only one of many women the Matrimonial Correspondence Club has represented. Answer me that."

"Yes, Your Honor, there were many others."

"Well, then, there you are," said the judge, smugly.

With obvious reluctance, Sutherton continued. "The owner and sole employee of the Matrimonial Correspondence Club is a woman named Deborah Pence. On the basis of information provided by me, the police in Chicago paid her a visit. Someone tipped her off, however, and before they could break down her door, she burned in her stove any incriminating records she had. The police told her of the evidence against her, and, in an attempt to gain some leniency, she confessed everything. She said the woman's real name was Priscilla Stull. She was, as I had suspected, Jack Stull's sister. Miss Pence also implicated an attorney who had handled the legalities for Priscilla Stull, dealing with the heirs and lawyers of her victims on her behalf. Miss Pence claimed not to remember any of the specific details in the destroyed records regarding Priscilla and her victims, but she did say that Priscilla had been corresponding with yet another well-off, matrimonially inclined, older gentleman. However, she could not recall the gentleman's name or where he lived. She said that information had been among the papers she had burned."

"Mr. Sutherton," said Judge Markham, "in my court, if a case is brought before me with no better evidence than what you have presented just now, I throw it out. I confess—and Marshal Pitts, I will ask you as a long-time friend to keep this information to yourself—I confess that I did write to the Matrimonial Correspondence Club. It is a little embarrassing, but it is in no way a crime or a sin."

"Certainly not," affirmed Sutherton.

"Not one little bit," said the marshal.

"I assure you, no one is accusing you of even the slightest indiscretion," said Sutherton. "But, if you will indulge me, Your Honor, I will finish my story."

"Very well," said the judge, folding his arms on his chest, and compressing his lips tightly above his out-jutted jaw.

Sutherton said, "I lacked that final piece of information, and when I received the telegram telling me Deborah Pence had burned it, I knew I had to do something. Jack Stull was dead, and I knew Lorna Fergin was away on some sort of business. You see, I had hired a man to watch her movements any time she was in town. So, I rode out to the Lazy 8 late that very night, and, carrying my boots in my hand, I sneaked into the house. I found Lorna's desk, and I searched it. I searched it thoroughly, every nook and cubbyhole." He paused to look at his two listeners, as if expecting a question.

The judge no longer seemed inclined to speak.

The marshal asked the question, "Didn't the woman lock her doors?"

"She did," said Sutherton. "Her doors, and also her desk." He smiled somewhat sheepishly. "In my former occupation, I had need, on occasion, to overcome the obstacle of locks. I received some training many years ago from a man who was . . . how shall I say it? Something of an expert in that field."

The marshal smiled and nodded in comprehension.

The judge's face was like stone.

"At any rate," continued Sutherton, "in her desk, carefully hidden, I found what I was looking for." He stopped speaking again, looking down at the floor, acting suddenly reluctant to continue.

After a few moments, sounding somewhat irritated, Judge Markham spoke. "Well, what was it, man? Speak up."

Sutherton looked at him, his expression neutral. "It was the name and location of the woman's next victim. It was in a letter she had received from Deborah Pence. I have it here." He reached into his shirt and withdrew an envelope. He held it hesitantly for a moment, and then handed it to the judge, who at first declined to receive it. Finally, he took it and, with trembling hands, opened it. His normally ruddy countenance reddened more deeply as he read.

Finished, he refolded the letter, inserted it into the envelope, and gave it back to Sutherton, saying, "This only proves that Lorna Fergin, or whatever her name is, had information about me. I still do not believe she is my Molly."

"Your Honor, you just put your finger on the reason I came here. I knew what Lorna Fergin looked like. I had seen her in town a few times. I figured that if I came here and found the woman who was coming to marry you, and she was Lorna Fergin . . . well, that would prove everything."

Suddenly, the judge sprang out of his seat, having realized something horrible. "The woman you killed. Are you saying she was my Molly?"

"The woman I killed was Priscilla Stull, who had been masquerading as Lorna Fergin. Only you can tell us if she was your Molly."

The judge looked at Marshal Pitts, panic in his eyes. "Where is she?"

"She's at the undertaker's place."

The judge left the room on the run, his short, pudgy legs flying. Sutherton and the marshal followed.

For obvious reasons, the undertaker's parlor was always open, the undertaker or an employee always present. The judge pounded furiously on the door, and shortly, it was opened. The judge said, "The woman who was shot tonight, where is she?"

The three men were taken to the back room, where on a metal table lay a shroud-covered figure. The undertaker helpfully held a candle above the scene as the judge reverently pulled the shroud down to reveal the face. He froze. For a long moment, he did not move or speak. At length, with wet eyes, he turned to face Sutherton, and he cursed him, wishing for him the deepest pit of hell. Then, he lowered his head and, murmured, "And thank you."

Sutherton and Pitts accompanied the judge all the way to his house, where he went inside, no words having been spoken since his final outburst at the undertaker's parlor. Marshal Pitts followed him inside, telling Sutherton to wait there.

Sutherton heard the marshal ask a question, and he heard the judge answer, "Let him go."

Outside, the marshal asked, "Where are you staying?"

"The hotel across from the station."

"I'll walk with you. It's on my way."

They walked in somber silence for a while, and at length, the marshal said, "I guess he was going to marry her."

"That's why she was here."

The marshal nodded and said, "Just out of curiosity, how'd it happen?"

Sutherton turned to face him. "I want you to know I didn't go to her hotel room with the idea of killing her. I knocked on her door, and she recognized me when she opened it. She seemed a little nervous, but she covered it. We talked for a minute, there at her door, and she invited me into the room. That was when I made my mistake."

"What mistake?"

"I called her Priscilla."

"I see."

"Before I knew it, her hand flashed out with that little .38 pistol, and next thing I knew, I had pulled my gun and shot her. I'm a gunman, marshal; it was pure reflex."

"Sounds like self-defense to me."

"It was."

"Why didn't you tell me that in the first place?"

"Would you have believed me?"

"No."

CHAPTER 16

The police chief had decided to handle this one personally. It was far too interesting to delegate to someone else. The locksmith was working on the lock and had been doing so for over twenty minutes, looking up periodically to say, "It's a special kind of lock."

After forty-five minutes, the chief wrote a message on the little pad he carried in his pocket and gave it to one of the uniformed policemen who had accompanied him. It took over an hour, but the man returned with another man, who was dressed in prison stripes and wearing handcuffs.

"Hello, Larry," said the police chief.

Larry grinned, displaying his three remaining teeth, and said, "Wot's afoot, Chief?"

The chief gestured toward the exhausted locksmith and said, "You can use his tools. Open that lock."

Larry walked over to the door and examined the lock. He held out his hands, and the handcuffs were removed. He sorted through the locksmith's tools, and made his selections.

Two minutes later, the door was open.

The chief went in first, holding a candle, though, with the door open, there was plenty of light coming in. The bodies were still positioned as Priscilla Stull had left them, though they had decomposed. Ed Macon's remains were lying on the floor, and those of Priscilla's stepmother were still strapped in the chair, opposite the portrait of Priscilla that hung on the wall of the mausoleum.

"I don't think Willie and me will be needing milk from your cow anymore," said Kyle Rupp. He had ridden over to speak to Sutherton.

"Why's that?" asked Sutherton.

"I'm going over to Proctor's to get our cow."

Kyle had previously told Sutherton the story of how Carl Proctor had cheated Willie out of the cow, and of his humiliating experience with Proctor when he had gone to get her back. Sutherton saw that Kyle was wearing his pistol. He looked at the gun and said, "Son, you won't need that."

Kyle looked at him questioningly.

"You needed it with Trey Paxton. Now put it away. Keep it handy, but put it away."

"Proctor won't respect me if I don't have a gun."

"No one respects a gun; they only fear it. It's not the gun that commands respect, it's the man."

Unarmed, Kyle rode up to the proctor place and hailed the house. Carl Proctor came out on the porch. Unlike the last time Kyle had come here, Proctor was not wearing a gun.

"Evenin,' Carl," said Kyle.

"Evenin'."

"I'd like my cow back."

Proctor looked away. "Figured that." He drew a deep sigh, looked back at Kyle, and said, "Well, I guess you'll never stop houndin' me about it until you get her, so go ahead."

Nate Tennet was on his way to the Longhurst's place when he saw a horse and rider approaching. As they drew near, he recognized Julia. He hadn't seen her since the day of the gunfight with Ramsey. He had, however, sent her a note explaining that he would be away on business for a few days, and would come and visit her on the evening of the day of his return, which was today.

He wondered if she was merely on one of her frequent rides, or if she had become impatient and come looking for him. He hoped it was the latter.

She reined in and said, "Howdy, stranger."

He smiled and said, "You're the prettiest thing I've seen all week."

They rode side-by-side and talked. She said, "Have you gotten your house put back together?"

"As good as a man can make it. It won't be pretty until you come and fix it up."

"Why, Mr. Tennet, that's an inappropriate suggestion. I could never set foot in that house, being an unmarried woman."

He feigned surprise. "You're an unmarried woman? I had no idea. We'll have to do something about that."

"If that's a proposal, Mr. Tennet, I suggest you make it a little more formal than that."

He reined in his horse, leaned over, took her in his arms, and kissed her. When he was finished, he said, "How's that?"

She put her head on his chest and said, in a soft, contented voice, "It's a good start."

End

MORE FROM THE AUTHOR
amazon.com/author/cmcurtis

FOLLOW C.M. ON FACEBOOK
facebook.com/authorcmcurtis

Made in the USA
Columbia, SC
10 December 2017